S0-BFD-701

ALSO BY CHRISTOPHER ISHERWOOD

NOVELS

A Meeting by the River

A Single Man

Down There on a Visit

The World in the Evening

Prater Violet

Goodbye to Berlin

The Last of Mr. Norris

All the Conspirators

AUTOBIOGRAPHY

My Guru and His Disciple

Christopher and His Kind

Kathleen and Frank

Lions and Shadows

BIOGRAPHY

Ramakrishna and His Disciples

PLAYS (WITH W. H. AUDEN)

On the Frontier

The Ascent of F6

The Dog Beneath the Skin

TRAVEL

The Condor and the Cows

Journey to a War
(with W. H. Auden)

COLLECTION

Exhumations

TRANSLATIONS

The Intimate Journals of Charles Baudelaire

(and the following with Swami Prabhavananda)

The Yoga Aphorisms of Patanjali

Shankara's Crest-Jewel of Discrimination

The Bhagavad-Gita

DIARIES

Diaries: Volume 1, 1939–1960

The Sixties: Diaries 1960–1969

Liberation: Diaries 1970–1983

THE MEMORIAL

THE MEMORIAL

PORTRAIT OF A FAMILY

Christopher Isherwood

FARRAR, STRAUS AND GIROUX NEW YORK

Farrar, Straus and Giroux
18 West 18th Street, New York 10011

Printed in the United States of America
Published in 1988 by Farrar, Straus and Giroux
This paperback edition, 2013

Library of Congress Control Number: 87003540
Paperback ISBN: 978-0-374-53346-5

www.fsgbooks.com
www.twitter.com/fsgbooks • www.facebook.com/fsgbooks

1 3 5 7 9 10 8 6 4 2

TO MY FATHER

BOOK ONE

1928

I

"No, not really," Mary was saying. "No, it didn't really help things much."

The doors were ajar. Anne, sticking entertainment-tax stamps on to green and orange tickets, listening to her mother's rich lazy ironical voice, frowned.

Mary was describing over the telephone, for the twentieth time, the awful scare they'd had at last week's concert, with the Spanish Quartet. The 'cello and second violin—poor little things, they were almost in tears—had left their parts of the Dohnányi locked up in a hotel at Victoria, and when Mary had gone round there in a taxi with only a quarter of an hour to spare, while they played the Schubert, she'd had the most terrific job persuading the staff to let her into the rooms. And, of course, it had all been very funny. Very, very funny, thought Anne, frowning. Very funny indeed.

"Ah, well; ah, well. That was just one of the awkward bits."

How Mother loves all this. And why shouldn't she? Anne's eyes moved round the attractive little room, with stacks of papers everywhere, the Breton armoire, the Steinlen poster on the wall, the bed, the dressing-table, the shelf of yellow paper-bound books, the gay chessboard curtains at the windows. Rather like the inside of a caravan. At night you went to bed on the camouflaged divan surrounded by the day's débris—letters, newspapers, press cuttings, other people's musical instruments, tennis rackets, and usually a little dirty crockery or a few beer glasses which had escaped notice in the wash-up after a picnic meal. And this is my home, Anne thought.

The truth was, she was still feeling a bit peevish at having had to move into the music-room, because of a Central School student whom Mary had invited in to sleep for the next fortnight, until she could get digs. The bed in the music-room had hot pipes running along the wall beside it. One woke up in the morning half-stewed. Why couldn't the wretched girl have known beforehand and made her own arrangements? But nobody ever knew anything beforehand here. Always these last-moment decisions, rushings out to get food, collect people for a party. Always this atmosphere of living in a railway station—just for the sake of living in a railway station. Anne yawned. But I quite see what fun all this is for Mary.

"Yes. We were bidden to a rich supper at the

Gowers'. My dear . . . I ain't proud, 'cos Ma says 'tis sinful—but of all the . . . yes, you've said it. . . ."

Not that she didn't work, harder than any office clerk, at her endless letters, which she answered in a great sprawling hand full of spelling mistakes. And the hours she spent at the Gallery, on a hard chair. And then having to sally out in the evenings to studio parties, concerts, shows at clubs, in order to meet, amidst the crush in the artists' room, some person who might, remotely, be "useful." Never tired, always ready to dance, drink, give imitations of Sir Henry Wood or Harriet Cohen, help cook somebody else's dinner, sing:

> Late one night, at the theatre,
> See him sitting in the stalls,
> With one hand upon his programme——

Your Mother's wonderful, they said. Anne had heard it all her life. Your Mother's wonderful. It was quite true.

And feeling this, Anne smiled with real affection at Mary, who appeared in the doorway, smiling, her hands full of papers, wearing an apron, a cigarette in her mouth.

"Did we send Mrs. Gidden her membership card?"

"Yes, I think so."

"She's just written to say she hasn't got it."

"Wait a minute, then, I'll look it up . . . yes, we did."

"The bitch!"

With indolent, unhurried movements, Mary added her papers to the pile on the table, selected others, copied an address into the members' book and strolled out.

The truth is, thought Anne, just avoiding sticking two stamps on to one ticket, I don't belong here. I'm not one of the Gang.

Yes, she'd felt it often. At charades, only a week or two ago, when they'd done the Ballet scene, and Edward had literally stood on his ear for about fifteen seconds. She'd found herself watching them, as though they were strangers. The curious thing is that Maurice belongs. It isn't merely a question of not being arty.

It wasn't that she was jealous of Mary. Not simply that. Though, of course, I am, slightly. She's awfully good to me. No, much more than good—really decent. Perhaps I should get on better as a lady. Living with Aunt Lily. God forbid.

I shall never be a tenth of what Mother is, thought Anne. And I don't want to be.

"Mrs. Oppenheimer wants two guest-tickets for a daughter and friend," called Mary from the next room.

"Right you are."

"I think the friend must be that plaintive little thing we saw at the Aeolian."

"Very likely," Anne called back, reaching for the tickets and entering them in the book.

If one had to criticise Mary, one could say nothing, absolutely nothing. She was above criticism. But must you always—Anne could sometimes have yelled out—must you always be so tolerant? Had Mary ever, during her whole life, had any really absurd, old-fashioned, stupid prejudice? Had she ever hated anybody? Had she ever really felt anything at all? One could hardly imagine it. Her utmost commendation of anyone: "That's a good number." Her utmost condemnation: "Your taste, not mine." She laughed things away—Bolshevism, Christian Science, Lesbians, the General Strike—"Not really very cosy," or, "I couldn't really fancy it meself."

I suppose I ought to go into a convent. A year ago Anne had seriously considered becoming a hospital nurse. She'd made enquiries, even tentatively mentioned it to Mary. And it was Mary's indulgent, ever so faintly amused smile that had made her feel: No, never. She couldn't. She could never face the Gang, who, with their little jokes, could turn it all into just one more new sort of game. The questions they'd ask. "Isn't it frightfully thrilling?" "Isn't it simply terrifying?" "Isn't it tremendous fun?" I suppose I'm just being romantic and schoolgirlish. I used to want to be Joan of Arc. It's all Sex. Good old Sex. I'm being screamingly funny. But I do long, *long* for someone who hasn't got this tremendously highly developed sense of humour. She thought at once of Eric. No, Eric wouldn't laugh.

There was the telephone again. Mary in the doorway, smiling: "For you."

Anne got up, felt herself beginning to blush, frowned, walked through into the other room. Should she shut the door? Damn it, no.

And as she picked up the receiver, her voice seemed to go suddenly out of her control. Smooth, false, clear as crystal, she drawled:

"Hul*lo*, Tommy. How goes it?"

The anxious little voice at the other end made her smile faintly to herself.

"Oh, my dear, *did* you? But how *too* thrilling.... How too splendid.... But that sounds most exciting. I'm sure I should love it.... Wait a minute, my dear, I'll just look and see. I'm not abso*lute*ly sure...."

She turned, to catch sight of her flushed cheeks in the mirror. Should she? Would it be amusing? Oh, well, yes. She sighed. Not exactly from boredom. Tommy always made her feel—responsible.

Out of bravado, she looked into the other room, where Mary was getting on with the tax-stamps.

"Is there anything special on, this evening?"

"No, I don't think so. I shall probably look in on Georges' little do. I might catch Hauptstein there."

"And you're sure you can manage with the rest of the stuff for to-morrow?"

"Perfectly, thank you, my dear."

Mary smiled. Anne explained, with sudden exasperation:

"I'm going out to the theatre. With Tommy Ramsbotham."

"Give him my love."

Their eyes met. Unwittingly, admiringly, Anne grinned at her Mother, thought: You think you're so jolly sly, don't you?

"And do try," said Mary, "to find out something more about the second Mrs. Ram's B."

"I don't expect Tommy knows much."

"Perhaps the whole thing's just another Chapel Bridge fairy story."

"I shouldn't wonder."

"It certainly doesn't sound like our Ram."

* * * * *

And in due course Anne was plunging into a simple but very smart frock, touching her lips with red, powdering, slipping on her new shoes—the complete box of tricks. It was like packing up a parcel of presents for a child. Oh, she felt thirty-five at least—so sophisticated, so chic, so wearily false, so benign, so maternal, so—good God, yes—so tolerant. She peeped at herself in the glass. Whisked downstairs.

She knew the whole programme. It had been

repeated so often. Tommy loved doing things in style. It was no good fussing, or telling him that he was spending all his pocket-money. He did so enjoy it. Am I a fearful cad? she'd often asked herself, looking round some quite grand restaurant. She decided that she was, and had better get slightly tight. Of course, at the theatre, it would be stalls. She sat beside him, watching a revue, simply trembling in her eagerness to be amused, to show that she was amused. And how he laughed when he saw she was laughing. And if he started laughing first, he looked back, as it were, holding out his hand, imploring her to follow. And then came the interval, when he said very negligently:

"What do you think of it?"

"I think it's absolutely marvellous," she'd say, beaming super-gratitude at him, as though he'd written book and music and was taking all the parts.

"Not too bad, is it?" She could hear his joy, his pride in the revue ring like a telephone bell through his drawl.

And then she'd ask him about the office and whether the work was very hard and how he liked it. And he began to tell her, carefully and seriously, suddenly breaking off with:

"You're absolutely certain I'm not boring you?"

Her tone crossed its heart, kissed a dozen testaments. She simply couldn't be sufficiently positive:

"My dear, I think it's most *frightfully* interesting."

And then they'd go on to the little place he took such pride in being a member of. His only regret was that it wasn't naughtier. It had never once been raided. And here she was soon beautifully muzzy, giggling up at him as they swayed about the room. Now she didn't care if she was a cad or not. Part of the wall was made of looking-glass. She kept catching sight of herself. Really, she had to admit, those eyes were pretty striking—and how really exquisitely I dance. She sparkled at him. He was flushed with happiness. In the taxi coming home she'd fairly ask for it. He kissed nicely. Life is so terribly complicated, she thought, stroking his hair. I suppose I oughtn't to be doing this. Why the hell not? Oh damn, we're in the King's Road already.

"I say, Anne, you are marvellous."

"Good old Tommy."

When they arrived at the mews she generally had enough sense to insist on his keeping the taxi and going straight back to his digs. Otherwise, he got maudlin. To make up, she kissed him in front of the driver. I am a harlot, she thought.

And next morning, of course, there'd be the usual reaction. It wasn't fair. If he were just an ordinary young idiot—and she'd met plenty. But Tommy was different. He really adored her. What a pleasing thought. She couldn't help grinning as she pronounced the word mentally to herself. But no, it wasn't fair. It would be almost better if she were just a harpy, luring him on. But I am fond of him, Anne thought. That's what makes it so immoral. I blow hot and blow cold. If only the poor darling hadn't given himself away so completely. He would put all his cards on the table. He was utterly reckless. He liked to humiliate himself. And that made it so much worse for her. This fatal feeling of security made her tease, patronise him. She behaved vilely. And she knew that he went home and brooded over every word she'd uttered, wondering: Now what, exactly, did she mean by that?

The worst moments were his proposals. That was really the most exquisite misery. She suffered for him—pins and needles, daggers. While he explained his prospects. Gerald didn't care much about the business. And if he, Tommy, worked, it was only a matter of time—"I know it wouldn't be much of a life for you, up there," he said. Sometimes she thought him quite shameless, playing on her pity. He was so dreadfully constant. She felt that she'd really been his only love from the cradle—Gatesley was practically that—and would be till the grave. If only he'd flirt with another girl and I got to hear of it, Anne thought, I might be honestly jealous. Yes, I should be. And then we should have got somewhere. But Tommy had no guile. He just lay there and waited to be stepped on.

* * * * *

As the bus turned into Cambridge Circus, Anne saw him faithfully waiting, under the shelter of the Palace Theatre. And suddenly she had a most unpleasant, apprehensive, sinking feeling—worse than she'd ever felt before. It was as if she were going bad. She was neither chic, false, modern nor benign.

Oh hell, she thought—I'm afraid I'm not going to enjoy this evening at all.

II

THE little Society to which Major Charlesworth and Mrs. Vernon both belonged met once a week throughout the winter months. Every week it visited some monument or relic of old London—a church, a city hall, an Elizabethan gateway in the corner of a Thames-side goods yard. Its members were chiefly oldish single women, young board-school teachers with pince-nez, an occasional clergyman, scholarly and querulous, asserting himself at lectures—earnest, curious, simple people, making their rambles into a little cult, mildly pertinacious, not daunted by the jokes of draymen or the stares of guttersnipes, determined to see everything, but glad of their tea.

Ronald Charlesworth admitted to himself that he felt out of place amongst them. The obvious slight pleasure of the spinster ladies at having a military gentleman in their ranks added to his embarrassment. But he wasn't going to be put off. As a young man he'd stood a good deal of chaff from his brother officers because of his fondness for museums, art galleries, old bookshops. Now that he was retired, middle-aged, with the War over, he could indulge his hobbies in comfort. Every week he was to be seen, at the back of the crowd—because, with his height, he could see over them easily—slightly stooping, his beautifully shaped jaw somehow recalling that of a warrior in a Japanese print, listening to what was said with a proud, delicate humility, his hands crossed like a martyr's on the crook of his perfectly rolled umbrella.

Ronald's friendship with Mrs. Vernon had begun quite naturally, the first time she had attended one of the Society's meetings, some months ago. The effusive lady who organised the Society's affairs had introduced them. They chatted about the place they had come to visit, their eyes asking the question: But why are *you* here? Neither looked the part of archæologist.

In appearance Mrs. Vernon was no more than thirty, and yet a curiously mature air of sadness and quietness surrounded her, so that he knew, after a few moments, that she must be ten or fifteen years older. She seemed sad, even though she laughed and smiled and talked in a rapid eager way about old pictures and old buildings. Since he had known her, she had been dressed always in black, which accentuated the fairness of her hair and skin and gave her sometimes absolutely the look of a child.

After the Society's meetings came always the question of tea. Sometimes the places they visited would provide it, free or at a shilling a head; sometimes they had all to make for the nearest confectioner's. At such times, Mrs. Vernon and Ronald naturally drew together, recoiling, without snobbery but by natural instinct, from the rest of the party. They had plenty to talk about. First and foremost, their mutual hobby. Ronald was surprised at her knowledge. It was not great, but it was much greater than he would have expected from a woman. And her feeling for the Past, for the romantic aspect of History, charmed him.

From archæology, they passed over many topics. He discovered that Mrs. Vernon painted; had painted, rather. She had done nothing, she said, for years. Thus it came about that she asked him to her flat, to tea. The portfolios of water-colour sketches she showed, with many apologies for their faults, made him insist that she ought to have kept it up.

"I haven't cared to," she answered, smiling sadly, "since the War."

And at that moment, though she hadn't made the faintest movement, Ronald noticed on the mantelpiece a silver-framed photograph of a man in uniform. Mrs. Vernon had never spoken to him of her husband. Himself so sensitive, he recoiled immediately, blamed himself for his clumsiness in paining her with his questions. But she, as though guessing this and wishing to reassure him, had continued:

"My husband was an artist, too. He was far better than I am. I should like to show you some of his work."

How beautifully, he felt later, she had said this.

* * * * *

Though they met often, their friendship grew slowly. But it did grow. Ronald was as shy as a schoolboy. He foresaw or imagined the approach of a snub and drew back long before it reached him. He showed Mrs. Vernon his flat, his small collection of etchings, his few valuable books. They went together to hear lectures at the National Portrait Gallery and the Victoria and Albert Museum.

Lonely himself, having few friends even at his Club, suffering often from the after-effects of enteric fever, which he had developed during the Boer War, Ronald yet thought of Mrs. Vernon's life as being lonelier still. At times, he pictured her as a sort of nun. She seemed so serene and calm. Once she had told him smilingly that her maid had given notice and been gone a week. She had been living, she said, on fruit. She liked it. She was in no hurry to get another. Ronald had been seriously alarmed. He was sure that she would be utterly careless about food, perhaps forget to eat altogether. She might make herself really ill. She looked as fragile as air. Yet he dared not say anything, lest he should seem to intrude upon her life. It was only by casual and tentative questions that he later ascertained that another maid had been found. Going to tea with Mrs. Vernon a few days after this, he saw the new maid for himself and was infinitely relieved.

For some time he had no idea that Mrs. Vernon had a son. When she did at length refer to him it was quite casually, and yet Ronald felt at once that behind her assumed indifference there was a tragedy. She spoke about something he had done as a boy, and it was as if she were talking of someone who had died. Evidently there was some shady business. Perhaps he'd forged a cheque. Probably worse. Was living in disgrace. And it must have broken his mother's heart. Ronald was a mild man, but he felt himself utterly without mercy in his judgment of that young bounder, who'd behaved so vilely to her. The only thing that could be said for him was that he had the decency not to show himself.

She had spoken to Ronald on more than one occasion of an old house in Cheshire where, he gathered, she had stayed for some years since her widowhood. It was the house of her husband's people. She showed him some of her water-colour drawings of it. And now, she said, this house was shut up and empty, in the hands of caretakers. When she spoke of it, her eyes had tears in them.

Oh, it was cruelly unjust, it was fiendish that she should have so many sorrows to bear. She seemed to have lost everything that she'd valued in the world. And yet she could still be so sweet and gentle, without any bitterness. And he, he'd have gladly been flayed alive if that could have lightened all this sorrow for her by one particle. He grieved over her in secret. He dared say nothing, not one kind word even, for fear that she should be troubled or embarrassed by his interest.

Ronald, with his Japanese warrior's jaw, his ill-health, his etchings and books, could hardly remember that he had ever been attracted deeply by a woman. Except in a purely physical sense, and that was when he was quite a boy; tall, clumsy, ignorant, turned out into a barracks to make his way somehow, being a younger son. He had been a dreamer, then, from shyness. He had protected himself from all that dangerous, half-alluring, half-disgusting side of life by secreting around himself a shell of action, hardship, routine, friendships with brother officers who eventually married and asked him to be their best man. And from this shell of action he had preferred to watch women moving about on the edge of his world, like shapes in water, beautiful, mysterious, with waving tendrils and blossoms. But that was years and years ago.

Now he sat in the Club drinking Sanatogen and

hot milk, thinking with pleasure that to-morrow the Society would meet for its weekly excursion.

* * * * *

They met, that afternoon, in the grounds of the house they had come to visit, an old mansion in the far western suburbs—the country residence of a family which was just about to relinquish it. In a few months the low white building with its Ionic portico, its Queen Anne windows, its long vista of shaven lawns between high elms which did not quite hide a steady stream of cars and buses along the distant road, would be sold, the house pulled down, the land used for building, for allotments, for playing-fields. The boards were already up at the drive gates, and the old caretaker who received them seemed bowed with the sense of impending disaster. The whole spirit of the meeting was tactful and hushed. Permission to view had been obtained as a special favour. There were three Lelys in the long gallery and a landscape by Cotman. They would be sold at Christie's. Some wonderful Jacobean furniture. The family had been driven into hotels, on to chicken farms, away to the south of France. The caretaker was alone, waiting for the enemy.

As Ronald walked slowly up the drive, the moist gravel shrinking crisply under his feet, the air of the avenue, bare as it was of leaves, clammy—it must always be clammy in that low-lying spot—

he was filled with the oppressive yet faintly pleasing reverent sadness which he so often experienced on these occasions. Mrs. Vernon was standing on the steps of the house. She smiled.

"I've been waiting for you," she said.

It was not the first time that this had happened. It was, to him, one of the most charming intimacies of their friendship that she liked to see everything at the same moment as himself, comparing impressions and scraps of knowledge with him.

She wore grey to-day, not black. And this seemed exactly to suit the mood of the sad, cloudy afternoon and the abandoned rooms of the mansion, where chandeliers hung from moulded ceilings, draped in holland bags. Their visit was somehow like a religious ceremony, and their eyes met with the expression of people who regard each other for a moment in church. The caretaker's voice echoed dully down the corridors. Ronald and Mrs. Vernon addressed each other occasionally, in low voices, remarking on a piece of china or the back of a chair.

At length, when they stood looking out over the lawn from a window on the second storey, she said:

"I can't bear to think of all this passing away."

There was real emotion in her voice. It moved Ronald deeply.

"People want to destroy all this," she said. "But what have they got to put in its place?"

The courage of her reactionary romanticism

moved him. He was a reactionary himself, perhaps, but, reading the newspapers, he had felt a confused enthusiasm also for housing schemes, playing-fields, London as a garden city. He belonged to both camps. She did not. He honoured her for it. Standing at the window, in the waning afternoon, with her slight figure, her low voice, she seemed to be crying out against that distant stream of scarlet buses and dark closed cars sweeping by the gates. She challenged the future with an extraordinary passion of quiet resentment. There were tears in her eyes.

"They've got nothing," she said.

He mumbled some words of agreement.

Mrs. Vernon seemed pleased at his support. She smiled sadly and yet gaily.

"At any rate, they've got no use for us."

III

Coming down the gas-lit mews with three beer bottles under her arm, Mary experienced, as often before, a pang of love for her home. My dear little house, she thought. It was full of people. The front door stood ajar. Lights shone from all the windows. Odours of fish-pie met her as she set foot on the stairs—which were really only a very steep step-ladder covered with linoleum. Mary had once tripped and slid down them on her seat, shooting right out into the mews and the presence of several astonished chauffeurs, clutching a new loaf.

"You've left the door open, Earle," called Margaret's voice from above; "somebody's got in."

They peeped down at her:

"Oh, it's only you, dearie. We were afraid it was more uninvited guests. There's enough of us as it is."

"And to think," said Mary, "of your poor old Ma running all the way from the Goat in Boots because you'd left your key behind. I thought the music-room window was bolted."

"So it was, but that didn't deter our Maurice. He climbed the drain-pipe."

Maurice, in shirt-sleeves, waiting for Anne to tie his evening tie, grinned.

"Look here, my lad, you know I don't like my sanitary system to be used for your gymnastic displays."

They all helped to lay the table, pushing past each other in the narrow doorway, each carrying a single fork or a plate.

"Oh, children," said Mary, "it's very kind of you to help Mother, but, you know, I could get the whole job done in two minutes alone."

"That's all right. Just you sit down and rest, Granny dear. Somebody get Mary her Bible and her cashmere shawl."

"I say, we just *must* subscribe for one. Wouldn't it be *too* suitable for the Gallery? She'd be exactly like those dear old pets one sometimes sees in ladies' cloak-rooms."

Earle came out of the kitchen:

"Say, if you don't eat your pie soon, Mary, I guess there'll be nothing left but the fish-bones."

"Oh, Earle," said Margaret, "you mustn't guess so much, my dear, really. It simply is not done. In this country we confine ourselves to the direct statement."

"Oratio Recta," said Maurice.

"Oratio *what* did you say?"

"Oratio Recta."

"I don't think I like that expression at all."

"Where's Eric," Mary asked, "and Georges?"

"Eric rang up to say he might be late," said Anne. "He's got to go to a committee meeting. He says he'll probably take a sandwich and eat it on the bus."

"And Georges isn't quite comfortable about something in the Hindemith."

Sure enough, Mary could hear the sound of a violin coming up from underneath the stairs. There was a stove near the coal-hole door and Georges liked sitting with one leg on either side of it and practising.

"He's scared stiff," said Maurice.

"He's not half so scared as I am," said Earle.

"I expect you'll forget your Debussy in the middle and have to play 'Mary Lou'."

"Nobody would notice."

"Don't you get being so nasty, my boy," said Mary. "You ain't got no call ter be so bitter at your time of life, and you so 'andsome."

"I think Oldway would notice," said Margaret. "He'd write that Mr. Gardiner's tempo left much to be desired."

"Now, children," said Mary, "we must eat. Maurice, don't be a pig. If you're too proud to have your dinner with us, you can leave ours alone."

Maurice was at his usual trick of sampling the food. He licked his fingers.

"Yes, I'll pass that. But it's not so good as the

one we had when Edward was here. He's easily the best fish-pie maker we've got."

"You might tell Georges we're ready," said Mary to Anne, glancing quickly—she couldn't help it—at Margaret's face.

"Heavens, I must wash," said Margaret. "I'm simply *filthy*."

* * * * *

Eric sat at the card-table, murmuring:

"Only members sign. Please give up your guest-tickets inside the door."

Rich old ladies in black silk, with veils, assisted by artistic nieces, passed along the passage into the concert-room, complaining of the stairs.

"My dear, are you sure this is the place?" one of them asked, with distaste.

Lady Croker, always rude, said that the passage was too narrow. The headmistress of a large girls' school gushed to Eric:

"We're sure this is going to be a *real* treat."

An elderly colonel, sent by his wife, came out to complain that members were keeping as many as three seats for friends and putting mackintoshes on them. A small newly joined member couldn't believe that one was allowed to sit wherever one liked. Two or three men lingered by the door, waiting for their chance to ask Eric where the lavatory was. A flustered lady wanted to know:

"Can you tell me, will my membership card and

these three guest-tickets cover the next three concerts, if I bring a friend who had a half-season ticket last year but couldn't use it?"

Eric had to deal with all these people. Sometimes he referred them to Mary, who was standing just inside the door. He could hear her strong reassuring voice, soothing all these unhappy creatures, promising everything, anything:

"Oh, yes, I'm *sure* that'll be perfectly all right."

Students came from the Royal College, bringing gaudy cushions, knowing that they were too late for the deck-chairs. Pale cultured Jews, rich amateurs. An Oxford don. The critics, with peevish frowns of predisposed boredom, treading on other people's toes. A few millionaire bohemians, in suits of rough, baggy, expensive tweed. A French teacher of languages. A famous actress. A chemistry master from a public school. Fragments of talk:

"Yes, the Upper Sixth are doing *The Merchant of Venice* this term."

"Roy scored in the last seven minutes. At the end, I simply couldn't talk above a whisper."

"Oh, but you missed something if you didn't see the private rooms upstairs."

And now they were mostly inside. The chatter had died down. Clapping. Beginning of a Bach partita. Eric pushed open the door and came quietly into the concert-room. Mary made room for him in her corner, at the back. The concert-room was the Gallery. Bright canary-coloured nudes in stockings on striped sofas hung round the walls, alternating with rather scratchy still life, a plate of gritty-looking bananas or a knife, a folded copy of *Le Matin*, one kid glove. The rigged-up stage was backed by sackcloth curtains. Georges' huge body dwarfed the little violin, like an enormous mechanical appliance required to perform a very delicate and minute task. He held it with grotesque tenderness, like a baby, his double chin doubled against it. Earle, when he came on to play the Debussy Preludes, was very nervous. He sat down in a rapid, preoccupied manner and started without waiting for any applause, as though he'd just hurried back from answering the telephone to resume work. What a noise he could make! "I didn't know he had it in him," Mary whispered to Eric, at the end of the second piece. "The only question is: will the platform stand it? We ought to have lashed the piano down with ropes."

* * * * *

Yes, he really is my idea of a saint, Anne thought, her eyes resting on Eric's tall bony figure, there in the corner, by her mother. You could have put him straight into the Bible, just as he was, in his plain, but obviously rather expensive dark suit, with his metal-rimmed glasses and the odd pauses in his speech, relics of his stammer. He wouldn't be out of place. There was something ancient and sombre about him. And when he looked at you, you felt that he was absolutely honest and fearless and good. He had beautiful eyes.

Perhaps they were all just a little bit afraid of Eric—yes, even Mary. They showed it when they chattered to him and made jokes in their own language, trying to pretend that he was one of themselves and nothing to be alarmed at. They knew quite well that he wasn't.

And really, what did any of them know about him, that mattered? What had made him, for instance, at the time of the General Strike, throw up his whole Cambridge career just when he was doing so brilliantly and was the coming man, as people said, and take to this work of his? Of course, it was all perfectly splendid—so splendid that it made one feel a little uncomfortable and chilly to think about it. Eric certainly wasn't interested in politics any more. From something he'd once said, he seemed to lump Communists and Fascists and everybody else together in one heap. And now that he was rich, he was carrying on just the same. He must spend at least half the money from the estate on his various funds and societies and clubs. Wealth only made him slightly more remote from them—though he was very generous, and had taken to presenting Mary with bottles of her favourite brandy. How strange it was to think of him—their own age—being confided in and seriously consulted at committees and organising relief work and making reports. Fancy herself doing that—or Maurice either, though he was so very much the business man now. And Eric never forced his work on their notice. Indeed, he often apologised for it—as when he came for the evening and had to explain that he'd told somebody they could ring him up there at such and such a time. He was always busy.

I wish, thought Anne, I had the nerve to talk to Eric. A really good talk. I should—yes, it sounded rather absurd, but I should like to ask his advice. She felt she'd take what he said as a kind of oracle. About all sorts of things—well, yes—curse it—about Tommy.

* * * * *

"I'm relying on you, my dear, to make this evening bearable," Lady Klein was saying to Mary as the last of the audience filtered out. Eric, on a step-ladder, was helping Anne unpin the sackcloth curtains from the wall. Already, the men had arrived to fetch away the piano. Mary was tidying up, encouraging one or two enthusiastic younger members who had volunteered to stack the deck-chairs in the cupboard at the back, counting some money which she had illegally received at the door, for tickets, in envelopes.

"I'll do my best," she promised.

"And bring anyone you can. I must fly off. I'll tell the car to wait."

"More work for the troops," said Mary to Anne and Eric, when she'd gone. "Be little heroes, won't you, and help your old Ma?"

* * * * *

Lady Klein's house had no carpet on the polished stairs. A precaution, somebody said, against drunkards. In the drawing-room there were Ming horses, Chinese embroidery, lacquer, old glass and modernist lamps with petal-like brass shades, possibly designed to represent Mexican desert plants. In the dining-room was a portrait by John, and supper. Bowls of salad. A chicken or two. Fruit. Somebody was playing on the spinet in an alcove. Everybody was standing up. The whole company slowly and uneasily circulated, like granules in amœba. Eric had the feeling that he must keep turning round and round lest some kind of area of danger should form behind his back.

He talked to Priscilla Gore-Eckersley and Naomi Carson. Looking round, he saw Mary, like a veteran warrior at bay, amusing, single-handed, six or eight people. Georges was hemmed in by admiring women eager to talk French. Sir Charles Klein, a frank, simple man, came forward to congratulate Earle. He had been impressed by Earle's hitting in *Ce qu'a vu le vent d'Ouest*. "By George," he said, "I shouldn't like to pick a quarrel with you, young man." Margaret's laugh squealed out. And there was Maurice, just arrived, with the girl he'd been taking out to dinner. Yet another new one.

The women laughed. Priscilla and Naomi laughed, anxious to be amused, never amused. Do they despise me as much as I despise them, Eric wondered. The proud enemies, smoking, laughing. "It sounds *amazingly* funny." No, they were not to be despised. They are formidable, Eric thought. Tell me, what is it you want? he would have liked to ask Priscilla Gore-Eckersley, the biologist, who had done so brilliantly in all her examinations, who lectured at the London University. She was questioning him about the work in South Wales. He began to explain to her the system of food tickets given by the Guardians. Part of the groceries obtained with the sixteen shillings-worth food ticket, Eric explained, has often to be given to pay the rent. Becoming serious, forgetting the Kleins' party, he described, with brusque gestures, a town where fourteen of the nineteen pits had been closed down and thirteen shops in the main street had had to shut. Even the Chairman of the Board of Guardians was nearly starving. A man who owned four houses was starving because he could get no rent and because, as a householder, Guardians' relief was impossible. Everybody suffers. The children are tubercular. Families of eight share a room. The houses are mostly condemned. People live on bread and pickles.

She nodded seriously, moving her eyelashes. But why are we talking like this? Eric wanted to yell at her, becoming aware again of her half-naked body, cunningly concealed and revealed by the sex-armour, her Eton crop, her plucked eyebrows, her scent—Good God, why are you so dishonest? Quick, let's go upstairs. There must be a bed somewhere in this damned house. But no, she didn't seem to want a bed. Not with me, at any rate. Then why does she waste my time? He turned from her to Naomi, the less subtle whore, who had asked, smiling:

"Eric, couldn't you possibly get me a job in a Communist Sunday School?"

* * * * *

It was the usual cry. Somebody do something. The party was beginning to stick. Lady Klein looked grim. Charades were suggested, with enthusiasm. But nobody wanted to act.

"Mary as Queen Victoria."

"Mary as Queen Victoria."

"Personally, I've never seen this immortal performance."

"Oh, but, darling, you must. It's *classic*. Mary, do!"

"Mary, you must!"

"Don't let us go down to our graves unsatisfied."

"But you've all seen it," Mary protested.

"We all want to see it again."

"Very well. But I must have my full London company. Let me see, who's done this before?"

Various performers were present.

Yes, and Margaret was the lady-in-waiting. But what about Lord Tennyson?

"The heavy lead? Oh, that was Edward Blake. Don't you remember how *screamingly* funny he was in that beard, reading *In Memoriam*?"

"What a shame he's not here."

"Out of Town, isn't he?"

Well, at last they were all chosen. Lady Klein, beaming gratitude, conducted Mary and Margaret to one of the best bedrooms, loaded them with clothes, old lace, brooches, everything for make-up.

"Just use *anything* you like."

"Thank you so much. We won't be long."

Mary sat down at the glass and began doing her hair. Margaret was listlessly inspecting the pile of scarves and shawls. Abruptly she exclaimed:

"Why the hell doesn't he write, or something?"

Mary went on steadily brushing. She said soothingly:

"Edward was never a model correspondent."

"Oh, I know. . . . But this time it's different." Margaret's voice was shaking. "Mary, what do you think has happened?"

"My dear, what *can* possibly have happened?"

"Oh, God knows. Anything. Everything. In the state he's in."

Mary twisted her hair into a bun:

"We're certain to hear to-morrow."

"My God—I can't wait much longer."

Mary rose from the mirror with a sigh. Margaret sat huddled on the bed, her shoulders shaking with sobs. She was fraying the border of her handkerchief with her teeth.

"If you like, I'll tell them you're feeling a bit rotten. Eaten too much caviare. You stay here. We'll manage somehow without you."

"Thanks awfully, Mary. But I shall be all right in a minute. I am a fool to behave like this."

Mary rummaged in her bag:

"'Ave a drop of Mother's curse?"

Margaret gulped at the flask. Then she came over to the glass, dabbing at her eyes.

"Gosh, don't I look bloody awful?"

* * * * *

"I say, Eric. There's something I want to ask you as a very great favour."

The party was breaking up. Eric had watched Maurice telling his girl to wait for him for a second and come hurrying across the room. He couldn't help smiling a little in anticipation.

"What is it?"

"Well, you see, Eric, it's like this—you know I always get off very unexpectedly—to-day, for instance, I hadn't an idea until I saw my boss at half-past twelve that I could wangle a night in

Town—as it is, I've got to be back at the Works at nine to-morrow—and, as you know, it's nearly the end of the month and I don't like to keep asking Mary——"

"How much do you want?" said Eric, smiling.

"Well——"

He could see that Maurice was wondering if he still remembered that other little favour, not to mention a ten-shilling note, "just until I get change," the day they'd all gone out together in the car. Eric felt so sorry for Maurice in his embarrassment that he hastened to say:

"I'm afraid I've only got £2 on me and some silver. Will that be enough?"

Maurice's face cleared with relief:

"Rather. Thanks most awfully, Eric." He grinned and added, with an air of great candour: "I haven't forgotten the—the other, as well, you know."

Never mind that, Eric refrained from answering, lest he should hurt Maurice's feelings.

"And, of course, I'll let you have it first thing to-morrow's post."

"There's no frightful hurry," said Eric.

IV

As the maid brought into the dining-room a silver dish of chestnut cream, Lily was saying with a sigh:

"Yes, the days are really getting longer now."

Eric did not move. His mother did not look at him. She had placed the table-spoon and fork further apart, brushing the tumbler with her silk sleeve, making it faintly ring. A sailor was almost instantaneously drowned. The maid put the dish down on its little mat.

Eric looked at the ceiling. Lily piled up his helping, leaving only a few mouthfuls for herself. She began to eat, with the gestures of one who is never hungry.

Eric looked at the ceiling, at the sky behind the solemn window with its silver-blue silk curtains. He thought: Why need we go through this? Which of us wishes it? His brain was numbed by the warmth of the closed room. Smells of Old Kensington—rotted potpourri and cedar wood burnt on stoves.

He looked at his mother. She smiled. Asked:

"You like this, don't you?"

"Yes. It's my favourite pudding."

Her faint smile did not question the dullness of his answer. She is only, thought Eric, asking: You admit that I've done my part?

Bowing his head, his mind wearily answered hers:

You've done more. You've done everything.

The telephone bell rang. They heard the maid's mincing reply:

"Yes, this is Mrs. Vernon's flat."

"Is that someone for me?" Lily called.

"Yes, m'm. It's Major Charlesworth."

"Does he want me to speak to him?"

"If you could spare a moment, he says."

Lily smiled, rose. She disappeared into the hall. Eric sat listening to his mother's voice. It was quite changed in an instant. Her telephone voice. Gay, almost playful:

"Yes. Yes. Good morning! Yes, I'm going, certainly."

Eric took a nut from the bowl of fruit.

"Yes, I think your best plan would be to take the Underground to Mark Lane and a bus on from there. It puts you down almost at the door."

Back she came into the room. How strange. Eric had the faint, often repeated surprise of seeing that she had after all not turned into a young girl, to match that voice. Yet she did not seem old. It was difficult to see where her fair hair was mixing with silver. She smiled sadly and brightly:

"It's my little Society, you know."

She smiled. She asked:

"Why don't you come with us next time we meet? I suppose you wouldn't care to?"

"I'm afraid things of that sort aren't much in my line."

Touching the little bell-push concealed beneath the table, she asked:

"Would you like coffee here or in the drawing-room?"

Thinking: I shall be sooner away, he murmured:

"In here, if you don't mind."

The coffee things came in. Eric had the tray placed before him. Lily faintly smiled. Ritual survives, he thought. She values that. He placed the spirit-lamp beneath the flask of the percolator.

"You see I've got some new cups?"

"Yes."

"How do you like them?"

He looked at them dully. Cups, he thought. Cups.

"They're very nice."

She seemed pleased.

"I got them at that new shop just opposite the Bank. I don't know whether you noticed it as you came past to-day?"

"No, I didn't."

Lily sipped her coffee. She said to the maid:

"Just bring in the cigarette-box from the drawing-room, please."

It came in. The silver box with the signatures upon it in facsimile of the friends of Father's who'd given it as a wedding present. Inside it was an unopened cardboard packet of cigarettes.

"Those are the sort you like, aren't they?"

"Yes, thank you. They are."

He broke open the packet, lit a cigarette. He didn't want it. She said:

"Why not take the whole packet?" She smiled sadly. "They'll only get stale."

"Thank you very much."

Obediently, he put them into his pocket. She watched him smoke.

"Have you been back long?"

"Only three or four days."

Why do you ask all this? his mind appealed to hers.

"What part of the country were you in, this time?"

"In South Wales."

Suddenly, she gave a bright, quick, playful smile, like a child asking:

"Tell me the names of the places," then added, as though challenging him laughingly to refuse her: "I like to look them out on the map."

She was extraordinary. She could always astonish

him. He repeated the names dully. She repeated them after him, asking how they were spelt.

"And where shall you go to next?"

"I don't know," he lied.

She smiled. It seemed to him that she understood perfectly what he felt, had even taken a gently mocking interest in seeing how far he would allow himself, to-day, to be questioned.

The clock on the mantelpiece chimed. He pretended surprise, clumsily, unused to such manœuvres:

"I must be in the City in half an hour."

"Must you?" She smiled sadly. They rose. She asked:

"When am I to have the pleasure of another visit?"

He flushed.

"I may be going away again soon. I'll let you know."

"You mustn't come unless you can spare the time. I don't want to keep you from your work."

Again she was sadly mocking. But he would not reply. She asked, as though without object:

"Shall you be seeing the Scrivens before you leave London?"

"I saw them last night. There was a concert."

"Oh, how nice!"

Eric challenged the wistfulness of her tone.

"If ever you cared to come, I'm certain they'd give you a ticket."

"That's very kind of you." She shook her head, smiling. "But I'm afraid it would be wasted on me. I don't understand music."

"Neither do I." His sudden exasperation made Lily smile. "But that needn't prevent your coming if you'd like to."

"I don't think I will, thank you, darling. I very seldom go out in the evenings now."

Yes, actually, he could swear that it had amused her to break through his carefully and painfully prepared armour. His armour of politeness, mildness, dullness. She said very sweetly:

"You'll give my love to Mary, won't you, when next you're there? I haven't seen her for ages. Tell her that any time she cares to, I should be delighted to have her to tea. But, of course, I know she's very busy." Lily was helping Eric on with his overcoat. "I've nothing very important to do myself"—she suddenly uttered a quiet laugh—"and so I always feel I may be rather apt to forget how hard other people in the world are working."

She came with Eric across the little hall to the door of the flat. Her manner changed.

"I hope your landlady feeds you properly?"

"Of course she does," he forced himself to smile.

"And doesn't put all sorts of ridiculous extras on your bills?"

"No."

"Well, good-bye, darling."

"Good-bye, Mother."

He stooped and kissed her cheek. Had an impulse to bolt down the stairs. Rang for the lift.

* * * * *

Out in the street, walking fast, he thought dully: Why do I come here? What makes her wish to see me?

She can trifle with all this, he thought, in a sudden gust of anger. It costs her nothing. She doesn't feel. For her this is only pleasant, sad. It's a sentimental luxury.

No, he thought, that's utterly unjust. I'm a brute. I'm vile to her.

Darling Mother. Can't I help her? Must we go on like this? It seems so miserable and senseless. His mind ranged for solutions, followed the old circle. No, there's nothing.

Nothing, nothing, he thought—seeing a tram, people shopping. Sane women with baskets choosing fish, or materials for curtains. Sensibility is an invention of the upper class, he had read, had said. Suppose one explained everything to that policeman. Don't get on with yer Ma, eh? After all, some of it could be translated into that language. But he would expect a black eye to be shown him, or a bruise inflicted by a poker.

* * * * *

It was a lovely afternoon. He had vaguely intended a walk in the Park. But bright, clean Kensington, with its nursemaids and old ladies, so prim and cosy and well-to-do—no, Eric was still haunted by the memory of a Welsh village. The strangely compact blocks of cottages, like the keyboard of a piano, mounting the hill. The sombre and motionless headgear of the pits. Men lounging in groups at corners. The rain-drenched landscape. The grey sodden sky. No, he must do some sort of work. He'd go back to his rooms in Aldgate and write a few more pages of his report. Later, he might see how they were getting on with the new room at the Boys' Club. And he'd promised his friend the probation officer to see if he could trace an ex-reformatory boy whom they'd got a job as boots in a commercial hotel and who'd disappeared. His uncle, who lived somewhere in the neighbourhood of Hackney Marsh, might know where he was.

V

Edward Blake stood for a moment at the corner under the lamp-post, swaying gently on his toes. Behind him, the Tiergarten lay inky black. Patches of snow gleamed bluish round the feet of the bare trees. In the Sieges Allee the lights shone brilliant and hard as diamonds upon the icy array of statues. It was much colder than the North Pole.

Edward didn't feel the cold. He started forward again, his overcoat flapping loose around him, singing to himself. He was beautifully warm all over, and the thing which kept whizzing round in his head gave him a pleasant sensation of deafness which was in itself a kind of warmth, blunting the edges of the freezing outside world. For quite considerable distances he walked almost straight—then suddenly he made an erratic swerve, wandering to the brink of the roadway or stumbling up against the steps of a statue. Whenever he did this, he saluted or said: Excuse me.

Edward knew the statues well. Heinrich das Kind was of course his favourite, but Karl IV. was the one he really liked. Karl and he had something in common. Karl always looked as though he'd seen something particularly fetching on the other side of the road. When Edward reached him, he sat down for a little on the steps. Then he got up and wandered on.

"Well," said Edward, aloud, but not addressing the statues, "here I am, you see." For it had suddenly struck him—how queer; ten years ago I wasn't allowed to come down this road. Now it's allowed again. And in ten or twenty years' time perhaps it won't be allowed. How bloody queer. In 1919 we were going to have bombed Berlin. Mathematically speaking, there's no reason why I shouldn't be dropping a bomb on myself at this very moment.

Somehow or other he got across the Kemper Platz without being run over. He had a curious feeling, as though he weren't allowed to look either to the right or the left, was in blinkers.

He'd been walking for hours and his feet were tired. He'd been right up in Pankow and down through Wedding. He'd stopped at least twenty or thirty times for drinks. Well, he was nearly home now. In the Potsdamer Platz an omnibus bore suddenly down upon him, seeming to swim out of the darkness, waving its lighted fins. He had to jump for the pavement. Why, I might have been killed, he thought—and this was really extremely comic.

His hotel was in a side street behind the Anhalter

Bahnhof. Edward steadied himself, said *Guten Abend* to the girl in the office, took his key from the hook. He met nobody on the way up to his room. At this time, early in the evening, the place was very quiet. He flung open the door. It banged against the foot of the bed.

How extraordinarily bright the electric light was. Its reflection flashed from the mirror of the wardrobe and from the mirror over the monumental washstand. The room was warm. Too warm. Edward sat down on the bed. The brightness of the light made him dizzy.

He rose and opened his suitcase, which stood on a chair. Yes, they were there all right. The two envelopes lay on top of his folded clothes. He took them out. Miss Margaret Lanwin. Eric Vernon, Esq. He opened Margaret's first. Three pages of it. How beautifully it's written, Edward thought. How bloody lucky I wrote it while I was still sober. Dear Margaret—By the time you get this I hope you'll be thinking a little better of me than you do at present.

Damn these explanations. And they'll read it all out in court. I could post it now, though. No, Edward decided, sitting down on the bed, I can't be bothered. He tore the letter up slowly. But perhaps they'll find the pieces and stick them together. The Germans are said to be a patient race. Better burn them. He went over to the washstand for the soap-dish, dropped the pieces into it and set fire to them. Then he carefully took the ashes, opened the window and scattered them out. Better clean the soap-dish too. It might be a clue. While he was cleaning the soap-dish, he dropped it. It broke in three pieces. Oh hell, thought Edward. But it'll go on the bill. I suppose somebody'll pay the bill.

He opened the other letter:

"DEAR ERIC,

At my Bank there is a small black metal box. Will you see that *all* the papers inside it are destroyed?

I am asking you to do this because you are the only person I can trust.

I am leaving you some cash for your funds. Spend it as you think best. EDWARD."

Yes, that was all right. He put it back in the suitcase and closed the lid. Should he lock it? No. That would only make extra trouble.

On the dressing-table lay the card of the man he'd been to see yesterday. The psycho-analyst. Somebody had talked about him at a party at Mary's. He was wonderful. The best man in Europe. Had had great success with cases of shell-shock. Edward had thought: Perhaps he could make me sleep.

But, of course, it had been just like all the others. A darkened room. A man in cuffs. Questions about early childhood. There was a man Edward had been to see years ago, just after the War, who'd elicited with great triumph that once or twice, in 1917, Edward had as good as run away. He'd faked attacks of rheumatism, got several days' sick-leave. "And so, you see," the bright little doctor had explained, "we're at the root of the whole trouble at last. Subconsciously, you've never forgiven yourself. Now you must try to look at this reasonably. Think of your splendid War record. Everyone must have periods of relapse. We aren't made of iron. There's no disgrace at all. None at all. Under the circumstances, it was really quite natural." "Under the circumstances," Edward had replied, "I'm willing to bet they wouldn't have got you into one of those bloody machines at the point of the bayonet."

Yesterday, the doctor had been very hopeful. It seemed to him, he said, a perfectly plain case. Yes, thought Edward, and it'll be plainer still tomorrow morning.

And now he opened a drawer. Took out his leather collar-box. Undid the strap. The little automatic lay within a coil of collars. It flashed in the light. Edward took it out, weighing it in his hand. It was bloody small. Again he mistrusted it. Surely it couldn't fail? Not if I'm careful. But he wished he had his Service revolver. That would have made a good old mess.

Standing in front of the mirror, opening his lips,

pressing the stunted muzzle against the roof of his mouth, he posed. That was right. No, tilt it back a little. Must be very careful not to point it too far forward. He swayed. The blood was pounding in his ears. I wish I wasn't so drunk. No, better do it lying down. I shall be steadier.

Lurching slightly, he moved towards the bed. As he sat down he became aware of his coat. A pity to mess a good overcoat. He took it off, dropped it across a chair. Now. He sat down again, sank back heavily. Lay staring a moment at the ceiling. Raised the pistol to his mouth.

Should he turn the light out? No. He couldn't get up again. Couldn't move any more. If nobody heard the shot it might go on burning for hours. It didn't matter. They'd put it down on the bill. They'd put everything down on the bill.

He closed his eyes. Immediately the blood-beats in his head quickened to a smooth, rushing, roaring sound. Louder and louder. He had the feeling that he was losing consciousness. Dug the muzzle hard against his palate. Further back. No, it didn't matter. A tremendous roar. Like falling. The first time you jump with a parachute. Yes. Quick. Now. Raising himself upon one elbow, he fired.

* * * * *

A bright surface. Pattern of cubes. The bright edge intersected the dark. A solid oblong shape bulging towards the top. The wardrobe seen from the floor.

Edward blinked. His eyelids were sticky.

Periods of coma passed like clouds over his brain, lasting a few seconds perhaps, or several minutes. Periods of awareness of the intense brilliancy of the electric light. He blinked. Something moved above him. It was his foot.

He had fallen off the bed and lay with his head and shoulders on the mat.

Sending out cautious messages, he established contact with his right arm, raised it a little, let it fall. His left also responded. He put his hand to his lips, held it up to the light. Blood. Not much.

O Christ, thought Edward, I've mucked it.

He wondered dully how much damage he'd done. So far, he was not aware of pain. Only a dazed sense of nervous outrage, as though something inside him had been snapped off short, leaving a jagged stump. It made him sick and faint.

I've mucked it, Edward repeated to himself.

Consciousness sharpened again, and he collected his forces for a movement. One. Two. Three. He swung his feet off the bed. His heels banged on the floor. That was better. Next, using his elbows, he rolled right over.

His elbow rested on something hard. He picked it up, holding it close before him. It was the automatic. The muzzle was caked with blood. Looking at it made him feel extra sick, so he let it fall. Sick.

Yes, he was going to be sick. At once. On all fours, he scrambled across the room to the slop-pail—just in time. It was mostly blood. Ugh! Filthy! He rested, gasping, panting like a dog, his eyes full of tears. A few drops of bright new blood spilt from his lips on to the floor. But more did not follow.

Gripping the corner of the washstand, he crooked one leg under himself, rose.

Immediately the room and the brilliant light made a smooth half-revolution, like an oiled fly-wheel. Edward reeled and fell across the bed.

After this he lay for some time, perhaps a quarter of an hour, staring at the ceiling.

I've mucked it, he thought.

The wish grew inside him to rise, to get out of this place, into the air. Cautiously he sat up, steadying his nerves against the giddiness. It swept over him and passed. He rose to his feet. As he shuffled forward, his feet kicked the pistol. It couldn't lie there. Sitting down on the bed, he hooked it towards him with his instep, captured it at last. Bending forward very slowly, he picked it up, closed the safety-catch, put it into his pocket.

Again he rose. Carefully steering his body with his will, he crossed to the mirror. Stared at himself. He wasn't such a sight as he'd expected. There was a smear of blood on his cheek and a stain running down from the corner of his mouth. And his mouth was pulled rather sideways. He looked as if he'd swallowed a dose of some nasty medicine.

Turning, steering himself, he picked up his overcoat from the chair, let it fall. He hadn't the strength to put it on. He was shaking all over. Sweat ran down from his hair. Out. He must get out quick.

He made for the door, twisting the light off as he went.

There was nobody in the passage, though he could hear people moving on the floor above. He didn't care whether he met anybody or not. They shouldn't stop him. He groped along the wall. At the stairs, he nearly pitched head-first down. He had to sit on the steps for a minute to recover.

Fresh blood was beginning to come from his mouth. He fumbled and found a handkerchief, pressed it to his lips. He must hurry.

Nobody in the office. He stumbled against the door. In the street the cold gripped like iron. It cleared his brain. A passer-by glanced curiously at him, but did not stop. A taxi. He waved to it. It drew up. Where to? Edward suddenly realised that he was crumpling in his fist the psycho-analyst's card. What a joke. He gave it to the driver, who read out the address slowly. Edward plunged into the car.

A stab of pain like a hot lancet slid between his eyes. It had started. Edward uttered a groan and lay back, covering his face with his hands. The taxi swung to the right, to the left. He was, suddenly, horribly seasick, tried to put his head out of the window, failed, and vomited on the floor. The pain struck him again, turning everything black.

They were helping him up some steps, into a house. The taxi-man and someone else. Edward tried to apologise for the mess he'd made. Put it on the bill, he wanted to say. He only coughed. And here was his friend the analyst. He doesn't seem very pleased to see me, Edward thought.

They'd laid him on a couch. People moved about. There were lights and voices. Somebody was telephoning for an ambulance. Immediate operation, and a lot he couldn't follow. Hands sponged his face.

Well, thank God, thought Edward, they'll do me in between them, that's certain.

BOOK TWO

1920

I

LILY, with her feet up on the chintz window-seat, her cheek resting against the oak shutter, thought: How tired I am. How terribly tired.

It was past eleven, already. Kent, on the box of the victoria, drove round and round the sundial like a clock. The August morning was warm and heavy and moist. The elm-tops were steamy. The atmosphere was drowsy with inaudible vibrations of the distant mills.

Lily thought: It will be like this always. Until I die.

From right across the valley, overlooked by the other window of her bedroom, at the back of the house, sounded the thin wild mournful whistle of a train. A pang caught at Lily's throat and her eyes filled with fresh tears. I ought to be glad to think of dying, she thought. This moved her. She uttered a sob, but others did not follow. She wiped her eyes. Almost immediately she had put away her handkerchief, more tears began to trickle down her face.

This year she had taken more and more to crying when alone. It was becoming easy, a habit. She knew this and must stop. Somebody, or several people, had told her to be brave. Be brave, she repeated to herself. But now that word had no meaning. It sounded rather idiotic. Why should I be brave? Lily thought. Who cares whether I'm brave or not? I'm all alone. Nobody understands or cares. She let the tears stand in her eyes, run down her cheeks, spill into her lap. While the War was still on it had been different. She could be brave then. While the War was still on her grief had had some meaning. She was one of thousands. They seemed to be encouraging each other, standing together. There was patriotism and hatred. You saw cartoons in newspapers and posters on walls. Lily reminded herself that all these mothers and widows, or nearly all of them, were alive to-day. But they no longer counted. No, we're done with now, she thought. There's another generation already.

And at the thought of this new generation, so eager for new kinds of life and new excitement, with new ideas about dancing and clothes and behaviour at tea-parties, so certain to sneer or laugh at everything which girls had liked and enjoyed in nineteen hundred—at that thought Lily felt not a pang of sadness but a stab of real misery. She was living on in a new, changed world, unwanted, among enemies. She was old, finished with. She remembered how, in schoolroom days, she and a friend had giggled at their middle-aged governess.

"You must try to live for your boy," somebody had written. Darling Eric, thought Lily mechanically. She always thought of Eric as darling, and her voice, saying the word, was almost audible to her. People didn't understand in the least. How on earth am I to live for Eric, thought Lily, when he's away at school eight months of the year? He was so young, too, when Richard was killed. We could never share this together.

She tried, all the same, to remember fresh scenes of Eric's childhood and boyhood. She saw him running about the garden on a day like this, five years old, in his red jersey and little spectacles. Poor Eric. Poor darling. He was always so plain. He didn't in the least remind one of Richard. Perhaps he was a little like dearest Papa. Lily smiled tenderly to herself and glanced out of the window. But the cockade of Kent's shining black top-hat still moved round and round the sundial. They would all be late. And then she had another memory of Eric, in his preparatory school Norfolk suit, with his new bicycle and another pair of spectacles, really hideous ones, made so as not to mark the bridge of his nose.

Of course darling Eric would be the greatest joy to her always and the greatest comfort. And every year he would be older and more able to be a companion to her. But the word "companion" stabbed through her again. A person who held your knitting. That's not life, Lily cried out to herself. That's not life; people being kind to you and talking in gentle voices, trying to think of things which will amuse you. That's not life. She got up, and, walking towards the other window, looked out across the valley at the hills towards Yorkshire and the chimney of the bleaching works by the river and the eye-sore, the new sanatorium for consumptive children from the Manchester slums. "That eye-sore," she called it fiercely, to her father-in-law, who, as usual, grunted. But my life is over, Lily thought.

Perhaps from this very room the Vernon girl of the story had seen her lover drown. Two tiny figures in the valley below. She must have had a telescope. No, it was absurd. The tall stalk-like chimney trailed a long wavy smudge of smoke across the sky. Turning away from that view, so terribly nostalgic, Lily faced her bedroom, the remains of her life; the silver-framed photograph of Richard, taken just before he sailed for France, the hairbrushes she had had as a wedding-present, the black silk cloak—part of her uniform as a widow, laid out across the foot of her single bed.

A friend of hers, who had lost her son at Arras, had tried hard to persuade her to go to a woman she knew of in Maida Vale. Not séances, just you and she together, and the room wasn't even darkened. This woman had worked in a shop. She was quite uneducated. Her control was a Red Indian. Lily's friend said how weird it was to hear her, when she was in a trance, bellowing in a deep man's voice and shouting with laughter. She was very small and fragile. It seemed that the Red Indian had told Lily's friend that her son was happy and waiting for her to come to him. The poor mother had been so much cheered. It was pathetic. But Lily couldn't believe. No, not in the Red Indian, at any rate. It seemed that there were some things we weren't meant to know. One reads books like the Gospel of the Hereafter and everything seems so certain and beautiful and comforting. And then you try to go one step further, and there is only mockery and blackness.

Yet the temptation was very strong and it was always present. Suppose one went to that woman and did get a message—just a few words, anything, so long as you could believe it was real. Suppose some woman held your hands and began speaking to you in your husband's voice. In Richard's voice. It would be ghastly, wonderful. One might walk out of that room and never feel unhappy again. Or perhaps, Lily thought, I should go straight home and drink something to send me to sleep. Then we could be together again at once.

Some time ago another friend had impressed Lily very deeply by describing how she had seen her dead husband standing, quite plainly, at the top of the staircase in her own house. Lily's friend had had no doubt whatever that it was really he, that he had come to console her, to show her that he was still alive in another world.

Lily thought a great deal about this. Finally, she knelt down and prayed that Richard might appear to her. She made this prayer for several nights. During the earlier part of the War, when Richard was still alive, she had prayed regularly for his safety. Nearly everybody prayed then. But since his death she had said a prayer only occasionally, or in church. Several days passed. And then one evening, as she was coming up the staircase from the hall to dress for dinner, she saw Richard standing in front of her. It was getting rather dark, and he appeared, strangely distinct, within the archway of the corridor. He was as she had last seen him, on his last leave, a slightly bowed figure in the British Warm and frayed tunic, his mild eyes wrinkled like his father's, but prematurely, with his deeply lined forehead and large fair moustache. There he was. Then he was gone. Lily, who had paused for a moment on the top step of the staircase, walked dully past the place where she had seen him, and along the corridor, down to her room. For days she couldn't think clearly about what had happened. She attempted different moods, tried to feel that this was a sign, that at last she was calm, she was happy. But she wasn't. Doubts wearied her. She couldn't believe. She felt that what she had seen was a creation of her own will. She had done something base in wishing to create it. Then she tried to put it all out of her mind. She never prayed to see Richard again.

Yes, I'm terribly tired, thought Lily. I'm absolutely worn out. I must stop worrying so much. I've got nothing to worry about now. This idea was as painful to her as the others. Her eyes blurred again. Is this all my share of life, she thought? Gone? Twelve years of happiness; paid for more than twelve times over in agonies of waiting during those awful months, expecting always the War Office telegram which came at last. Killed in Action. Lily was standing in front of the looking-glass.

Her lips trembled; she was frog-faced, half smiling. Somebody knocked at the door. She sighed deeply. Her face drew down at the mouth and eyes. She looked five years older.

"Come in," she sighed aloud.

She picked up her hat from the dressing-table and put it on, arranging the little veil. The hat made her eyes look extraordinarily lost and tragic. She could still occasionally feel the pathos of the sight of herself in black—a small restrained figure beside which always stood, in her imagination, the charming fresh image of a girl in spreading cream skirts and a large hat with flowers, puffy-sleeved; herself as a young mother. The knocking, discreetly insistent, was repeated. Lily frowned and called sharply: "Come in."

"Master's just gone down to the carriage, Mrs. Richard. He told me to tell you to be sure and hurry, because it's getting late."

Mrs. Beddoes smiled with the privileged irony of an old servant.

Lily said: "I've been ready for the last half-hour," and she too smiled—a smile, as she suddenly felt—catching a glimpse of it in the mirror—of the most extraordinary pathos and sweetness. She saw the effect of the quick sad smile together with her slightly inflamed eyes on Mrs. Beddoes, who stood aside for her to pass with a certain added quality of respect. Respect for her grief. For the ordeal her feelings were about to undergo. Poor Mrs. Richard.

Lily passed quickly down the gloomy corridor on light footsteps, her cloak about her. A shaft of sunshine full of teeming motes struck down across the staircase from the small high mullioned window. The staircase creaked even under her weight. The heavy baluster-heads of carved oak fruit were nearly black with age. She paused for a moment, half way down, and stood, as she often did, taking in the silence and age of the house. The huge and faded piece of tapestry clothing the wall above her. The cheese-coloured ovals of faces painted upon wood three hundred years ago. The clock's tick like a man walking in armour. And as Lily stood there, she could feel so wonderfully calm and happy that it was like a kind of hope growing up inside her. She thought: No. I shall never forget him, never. I shall never forget our life together. I shall never forget how happy we were. Nobody can take that away from me. And after all, Lily thought, I shall be brave. It's quite easy. I shall be able to be brave and smile and be wonderfully sympathetic to every one, simply because nobody knows what my life with Richard has been. How marvellously happy we've been together. As long as nobody knows that and as long as I never forget what my life used to be like, I shall be quite contented. I shall be brave and I shall be safe, because nothing can possibly happen which will touch me again. Lily came down two more steps and now she was standing in the sunshine. She was standing there with her face lit pure gold, like an angel, when Eric came running up the stairs to fetch her. He was pale and breathless. She seemed to dazzle him.

"M-mm," he blurted at her, with his painfully uncouth stammer.

"Darling, you *must* remember to count before you speak. You're getting worse than ever."

"I'm s-s-sorry."

He stood before her, so uncouth, looking more than his height with his shambling limbs and clothes just slightly too small. Lily hated the bother of buying clothes and Eric never seemed to have any ideas of his own except negatives ones. Most boys of seventeen were so particular. Maurice had looked quite grown up when last she had seen him in his best. And it isn't as if I couldn't afford it, thought Lily. I really don't know how Mary manages.

"Because I'm perfectly certain, my darling, that you could cure yourself if you'd only fight against it. You mustn't just lose heart. Everything can be cured."

As she said this, stretching out her gloved hands to straighten his tie, her face was radiant. It seemed to her that by uttering these words she was confirming for herself the truth of what she had just been feeling. She looked tenderly into her son's eyes, through the lenses of his powerful spectacles. He had preferred steel ones to the much more becoming sort with horn rims when they bought a new pair last spring. She sometimes wondered whether he didn't take a perverse pride in looking as plain as he could. Smoothing his hair, she asked, smiling:

"Can't you really make it lie down better than that?"

He flushed, and she saw, with a strange sense of irritation, that she had made him feel ashamed of himself.

"I did t-try, Mums."

"Darling." She laughed gently, kissed him. "We mustn't keep Grandad waiting."

They went down, her arm beneath his, into the hall. Outside, in the frame of the porch, the garden looked brilliant. The carriage was standing at the door, and John Vernon's back, hoisted between Kent and Mrs. Potts, filled the whole space between the box and the seat as he paused in the act of mounting. They might have been handling a very large grey tweed sack, chock full, with its neck tied up in a white woollen muffler and a homburg hat perched on the top. Kent puffed, Mrs. Potts strained, they made a final effort. And the old gentleman, lifted by main force into the victoria, slewed round and sank heavily upon his seat. The springs of the carriage gave visibly on the far side. John Vernon's pink and attractive face, with its silver moustache and slobbery mouth like a baby's, was smiling with pleasure and amusement at his own helplessness and weight, at the trouble he had caused and at having got once more safely into position for the chief adventure of his day, his drive. His soft white freckled hand held a half-smoked cigar dangerously near his opened coat front and his broad waistcoat, covered with those little food-stains which were Mrs. Potts' despair; as fast as petrol could take them out, more were made. Mrs. Potts advanced, anxious about the cigar. She signed to Kent, who, understanding what was wrong, contrived, in tucking the rug round his master's lap, to prop up the hand which held the cigar away from the flap of the overcoat. At once Mrs. Potts was all smiles with relief, and now Mrs. Beddoes, coming out of the house behind Lily, joined her. Lily got into the carriage, kissing Papa good morning as she did so. She took her place beside him and Eric sat opposite. He was wearing his black school clothes and a bowler. They were all in black except John. Mrs. Beddoes had been sure the master would catch cold if he wore his top-hat. She and Mrs. Potts, grey-haired women in aprons, stood watching their master as the carriage drove out into the park. They came out after it to close the garden gates.

They both admire him tremendously, Lily thought. And with pride she reflected that her father-in-law had a dignity all his own. A dignity so intrinsic, so little dependent on outer appearances, that it could be appreciated by these two women who, for the last five years, since his slight stroke, had washed and dressed their master, performing the most menial offices for him, like nursemaids. There he sat, as the victoria bowled along the drive, across the bare stretch of the little park, broken only by clumps of bushes and small ponds, along the avenue of oaks, beeches and ash-trees, with his wide happy smile of contented ownership, looking at nothing, the cigar beginning to singe the fringe of the rug. He smiled as she moved it a little, smiling. She felt his hand to make sure that it wasn't cold. He gave a grunt.

None of the trees grew very high, because the park, although apparently so low-lying and even swampy, was on a higher level than the Cheshire plain, and the wind blew across it from the sea: perfect hurricanes in winter and even to-day there was a little breeze. Papa had a story that, in the days when he still went for short walks, he had met an American sea-captain in the park. The sea-captain didn't seem to realise that he was trespassing. He came there, he said, every day to get the air. It smelt, he said, of ozone. The finest air in the Midlands. Some people have cheek. There was a little ash-tree, planted the year Eric was born; and there, a bit further along, was another, planted on their wedding-day. And deliberately, because it gave her pain to think about it, Lily tried to remember a day even earlier, the day she had first come to the Hall. That was in the spring. And closing her eyes, she managed, for an instant, to see the park and the house as they had looked to her then, so different, yet really just the same as now, except that there were flower-beds round the sundial and the sycamore hadn't been cut down in the corner of the garden. But she didn't want to think of anything but the differences.

* * * * *

That evening Lily had knelt down in her dressing-gown with her elbows on the dressing-table, to get the full light of the candles burning on either side of the mirror. Opening the silk blotting-book, she continued her letter to her aunt:

"The house itself is partly Elizabethan. . . ."

She paused, looking at herself in the glass. Her eyes held tiny reflections of the candle-flames. They were brilliant with happiness. Her bright hair flowed over her shoulders, her cheeks were flushed. What a day! Her diary—which she would turn to next—allowed one page for each, and she had a childish fad of filling each one exactly by making her writing either bigger or smaller. This evening it would have to be very small indeed.

"The house itself is partly Elizabethan." Lily gazed into the mirror, into the shadows of the enormous solemn best bedroom, with high-backed cretonne chairs boldly patterned. A fire burning brightly—put in, she felt, more to make her feel cheerful than because the weather needed it—could not dispel those shadows, it only made them more grotesque. There was a woollen-worked fire-screen, so charming and amusing, a real relic of the Early Victorians. And on the mantelpiece there were the most absurd little china lambs, with rough china fleeces, which you could use for striking matches on.

No, Lily couldn't feel that this room was really gloomy. She'd expected—but already she'd forgotten exactly what she *had* expected of the Hall. Richard sometimes talked about it as though it were a perfect dungeon. And yet he was really devoted to his home; nobody could be more so. Of course, thought Lily, nothing could have seemed anything but perfect to *me*—even if it hadn't been; and it is!

". . . but it has been refronted," she wrote, with sudden decision, "and the mullioned windows on the right side of the porch replaced by sash windows, about the time of Mr. Vernon's great-great-grandfather."

Richard had been really amazed, and so pleased, when she'd asked his father about that, at dinner. Because, as he pointed out, she must have noticed it actually as they were driving in at the gates. They hadn't walked round outside at all yet.

"Lily notices everything," he had boasted, going on to tell them how she actually went into old churches — not during the service, of course— and took measurements with a tape measure, the length of the nave, breadth of the chancel, and so on, as well as making sketches of carvings and doorway ornaments, and put it all down in a book. "She ought to have been an architect," he went on, laughing, making Lily blush. But Mrs. Vernon had been so charming to her and so much interested, asking questions about St. Clement Danes and St. Mary-le-Strand. And then Mr. Vernon told her how some of the windows overlooking the stable-yard had been bricked up at the time of the Window Tax. Then he went on, speaking in his slow, rumbling voice, to tell a story about a Cavalier who had visited the house in the weeks before the outbreak of the Civil War to see his lady-love. The Vernons had stood for the Parliament. One night the lady-love's mother had discovered that the young Cavalier was carrying secret despatches; among them, her husband's death-warrant. When the Cavalier left the house next morning he was accompanied by a servant who was to show him the ford in the river. The servant, at his mistress's order, led the young man to a place where the current was strong and the water very deep. The Cavalier was drowned, and the girl, watching the scene from her window, was driven mad. "They say she haunts the wood behind the house. That's the reason it's called the Lady Wood," said Mr. Vernon, with his slow, very charming smile. During dinner he had drunk none of his wine. Now he picked up his glass of Chablis, his glass of port, his whisky and soda, his liqueur, gulping them down straight away, one after the other. At each gulp he blinked and smiled. And this, too, seemed charming and amusing to Lily. He was like a child taking medicine. And he was so kind.

But everybody had been kind. Kent, the coachman, had seemed to welcome her specially in the way he touched his cockaded hat, as she and Richard got into the carriage at Stockport Station. Stockport, Richard said, was a dirty old hole of a place, but she'd liked it as they rattled over the setts. Of course, it was different from the South; grey, smokier, barer than anything she'd seen in London—but she was determined to find some romance in it. And Mr Vernon had supplied that.

"They always say," he told her, "Stockport is like Rome—it's built on seven hills."

And then there was the long drive through muddy, twisting lanes, past straggling houses, across the high-arched bridge over a canal, grinding with the carriage-brake on down a steep little hill. Richard pointed out two or three neighbouring "places," standing in fields, among trees. The unfamiliar names thrilled her. He was holding her hand.

Mr. Vernon was standing in the porch as they drove up. He was not quite so tall as Lily remembered him—at her aunt's house in Kensington—but perhaps that was because the whole Vernon family were above the normal height. She kissed him, turning to the tall dark girl behind, who she knew, of course, must be Mary, and shook hands with her, conscious all the while of the hall beyond, with its flagstones, and the big porters' chairs by the fireplace and the old portraits against the panelling. Yes, Mary had Richard's eyes, they were beautiful, but she wasn't so good-looking. Lily liked her, loved her, instantly. She was shy, rather awkward. She seemed so big, to Lily. Ought she to have kissed Mary? They smiled. Lily had just that impression of those lovely eyes in the plain, rather pale face.

Mrs. Beddoes, the housekeeper, was introduced. And Mrs. Beddoes half-curtsied as she said:

"Welcome to the Hall, miss."

That was almost too exquisite for Lily. She nearly took Mrs. Beddoes in her arms. And actually she felt the tears in her eyes. They were all too kind. Mr. Vernon, tall, slow and stooping, with his fair moustache and mild wrinkled eyes, saying: "I expect you'd like to see your room?" And Mary, moving ahead of her shyly, at the top of the wonderful carved staircase which was sloping sideways with age, opening the door: "I hope this will be all right."

"It's perfectly beautiful."

They paused, smiled enquiringly. Mary smiled quickly, oddly. She had a most attractive voice—rather husky and soft:

"I'm glad," she said. That was all. They were interrupted by the gardener's boy bringing up the luggage. Mrs. Beddoes came in to begin the unpacking. The whole house was in a bustle.

"We've been looking forwards to this for weeks, miss," said Mrs. Beddoes, when she was alone with Lily. "So has Master and the Mistress—you wouldn't believe."

Whatever could she say? She'd wanted then, as later, when she took Mrs. Vernon's hands and kissed her, standing beneath the great glass chandelier in the drawing-room, to cry: Thank you, thank you—thank you for living in this house, for being so perfect. She would have liked to be absolutely schoolgirlish. But since she was grown-up and couldn't, she put on her nicest dress, the pink and silver, hoping it would please them all.

And now, what was she going to say about all that to her aunt: in her diary? She gave it up. To-night she was too tired. But she didn't go to bed at once. She sat staring at herself in the mirror, silly with happiness, the jewel of her engagement ring against her lips.

* * * * *

"It scarcely seems possible that I have been here only a fortnight to-morrow," Lily wrote in her diary later. "Drove up the village with Mamma and Papa in the morning. . . ."

They drove up the village most mornings. First they stopped at the grocer's, then at the butcher's, then at the fishmonger's. The shop-keepers came running out and stood bowing at the brougham window. At the stationer's, where Mr. Vernon got his tobacco and mystery novels, Mrs. Vernon and Lily were left to travel on alone, visiting various poor houses in the back streets behind the Wesleyan Chapel. Kent was sent indoors with parcels, and women came out to thank Mrs. Vernon, wiping their hands on their aprons. Lily wished that they would have curtsied, as she'd seen the villagers do in a village in Suffolk where she sometimes went to stay. It was the only thing she criticised about Chapel Bridge—the people seemed so very off-hand. Their bows were little more than nods. And the crowd of women in shawls and clogs whom one met trooping out of the mill at midday—they didn't even nod, they simply looked at you, not unpleasantly, but rather as if you were something in a museum. They seemed to take everything for granted. Once, this had struck Lily so forcibly that she had exclaimed in generous indignation, as they drove away:

"I'm afraid you're really too good to them, dearest Mamma. Unfortunately, that class can't always appreciate what's done for them."

Mrs. Vernon had extraordinarily delicate, pale Grecian features. Lily often thought that she was one of the most beautiful people she'd ever seen. She half-closed her eyes when she spoke:

"In this part of the world, my dear, one has to supply the appreciation oneself."

She lay, much of the afternoon and evening, on the sofa under the chandelier, in the drawing-room. Lily never heard what complaint she suffered from. She was simply fragile, as flawless china is fragile. Mary did all the housekeeping; Mr. Vernon brought her her books and papers from other rooms; she thanked them exquisitely by her mere gestures. She said:

"You all spoil me. I shall give you reason to regret it."

She lay with half-closed eyes, the white feather boa about her shoulders, wearing long gold ear-rings. And, as Lily looked at her, she sometimes felt an absolute awe, an adoration. Mrs. Vernon seemed precious and sacred, like an ikon. Lily was secretly preparing an offering to make to her, a book of sketches of the Hall. When they were finished, she would bind them herself. Book-binding was another of her small talents. Richard, of course, had to be shown the book, under strict promises of secrecy, as it progressed. He had seen all her earlier water-colours and sketches. These, he said, were better than anything else she had done. They were marvellous. Lily basked in his praises.

"How could they help being," she asked, "when everything's so perfect here?"

"Before you came, it was the dullest old hole you can imagine."

"You don't deserve to live in this house," she told him, half-shocked, "you can't appreciate it."

"You've made me appreciate it," said Richard.

The weeks passed into summer. Mrs. Vernon had come out of doors to lie in a *chaise longue* under the copper-beech on the Terrace. Her red sun-shade protected her from the strong light streaming down through the leaves. Lily sat beside her. They talked of Lily's childhood, her dead parents, her aunt—to whom Mrs. Vernon asked always to be remembered in Lily's letters—of the wedding in the autumn. They talked of Richard—"You must promise me to take care of him," Mrs. Vernon had said, and once: "My dear, how am I to forgive you for taking him away from me?" For Richard's work would be in London and they would live there, after the first year. But Lily answered: "You know, darling Mamma, that, if I could, I'd stay here always." Mrs. Vernon laughed and touched Lily's hand.

Once or twice a week they drove out in the victoria to pay calls. Often there were callers. The Wilmots drove over from Torkington, the Knowles from Mellor, bringing their visitors with them to see the Hall. There would be tea on the Terrace, and afterwards Mrs. Vernon would depute Lily—rather than Mary or Richard—to show them round. "Oh, she's much the best guide," she would say, smiling. "Lily knows the house better than we do ourselves." And so Lily, flushed with pride, would lead off Colonel Somebody or Lady So-and-So, beginning at the library and sparing them nothing, trying hard to communicate some part of her own glowing enthusiasm and sincerely vexed when the gentlemen seemed to prefer looking at her to examining the Blue Dash charger on the chest by the window. Once she went as far as exclaiming: "I don't believe you're attending to one word I say." The military man was all confusion: "Oh, I say, you know—dash it, ha ha, is that quite fair? I give you my word of honour. . . ." "You wouldn't have liked it," Lily cut him short with a smile, alarmed at her rudeness, "if I hadn't listened to all those interesting things you were telling me about the Boers."

On other days—and this amused Lily more than the County people—there were callers from Chapel Bridge itself. The vicar's wife came and the doctor and the manager of the bank. Lily described them all in her letters. She was seldom malicious, and could write quite sincerely that Mr. Hassop was "delightfully vulgar." She loved to see Papa strolling with him in the garden, chatting so amiably, offering him cigars. Mr. Hassop made her feel the prestige of the Hall in the village, among the churchwardens and substantial men. He spoke of Papa always as the Squire, Mamma he treated as a kind of Queen. And really, thought Lily, they'd make a most imposing royal couple.

That summer, in the hot garden, it had been like a world where nothing will ever happen. Mamma under the tree, exclaiming, as visitors were announced: "The Philistines are upon us!" Papa telling how an Italian coachman had jumped off the box and snapped Papa's walking-stick across his knee in a fit of temper: "And, if you'll believe me, he said neither Dog nor Cat—simply got back into his seat and drove as hard as he could go, down to the Villa." Richard's voice from the tennis court, calling the score. A beautiful, happy world, in which next summer would be the same, and the next and the next—the County gossip, the Balls, engagements being announced, girls "coming out," talk about the cost of keeping up one's place—the shooting, hunting, livestock—humorous allusions to people who'd made money in cotton—Mrs. Beddoes and the others passing between the tea-table and the cool house, with plates of cress and cucumber sandwiches. The old safe, happy, beautiful world.

* * * * *

Papa made a convulsive movement, as though to commit suicide by flinging himself out of the carriage. He was only trying to throw away his cigar. Kent climbed down from the box and took it from him, while Eric opened the park gates. Lily had seen Kent light Papa's pipes, taking several pulls first at the pipe himself and wiping the mouthpiece on the sleeve of his coat. Another of his offices was to cut his master's corns in his attic smoking-room with a razor. Now he stubbed out the cigar against the wheel. Lily couldn't be sure whether he had or hadn't slipped it into his pocket.

She looked at her watch, leant forward:

"I think we shall be just in time, after all," she said to Mr. Vernon, being careful to pronounce the words very distinctly.

"What?"

He did not say What, but Whuh—this being an easy example of the grunt-language, unintelligible to almost everybody but Kent, Lily, Eric, Mrs. Beddoes and Mrs. Potts—in which he now spoke, partly through infirmity, partly through laziness.

"I don't think we shall be very late, after all," said Lily.

Mr. Vernon gave his affirmative grunt. He smiled widely. He didn't care whether they were late or not.

And looking at him with tenderness, Lily well understood the admiration of Mrs. Potts and Mrs. Beddoes. She thought of his early travels. He had been all over Europe and to the East Indies and to America. He was never seasick—once, off Norway, the captain had challenged him to an endurance test—platefuls of cold mutton-fat—and lost. And on another occasion the whole crew had apologised to him next morning for feeling ill. He had proposed to Mamma seven times. He had played village cricket. Had spoken at the opening of Zenana mission bazaars. Had been a J.P. Had met Ford Madox Brown in Manchester and invited him over to see the tapestry. To Lily, he represented now the whole of the past—for Mamma was dead, Richard dead, her aunt dead—all that she loved and looked back to with regret.

But Papa could never have really understood Richard. She forgave him that. For nobody had understood Richard but herself. That was her pride and her consolation now. He should have been sent to Oxford or Cambridge and become a don, instead of going to Owens College and into that solicitor's office. Richard had never cared much for being a solicitor. His talents were quite wasted.

Nevertheless, some of the happiest hours of their married life had been spent in museums, libraries, churches. Richard developed tastes which must have been latent all the time. He began to sketch. He became good—better than herself. She was so proud of his work and showed it to everyone who came to the house.

Outside the park gates the village began almost at once, with the hideous new pink brick villas they were building. Most of them were bungalows. The windows were decorated with chessboard panes of stained glass; flowers and fruits. And if you looked inside you were confronted with an awe-inspiring varnished contraption of drawers, brackets, fretwork and looking-glasses, a super-sideboard, covered with photos and fancy china bearing the arms of seaside towns. How do these people live? thought Lily, with a shudder. Where is the romance? They passed the Ram and began to clatter on the setts. She went back to her reflections. The village street opened ahead, two lines of plain dark Midland houses, a few small sweetshops, pavement, lamp-posts, no trees, the mill against the sky. Suddenly, an idea which had been in Lily's head for a long time seemed confirmed. Darling Eric. He must fulfil what Richard would have wished. He must be a don. Everyone told her that he was so clever. His History master felt sure that he would get an entrance scholarship to Cambridge. Of course. How delightful that would be. How happy it would make Richard. And Lily saw herself walking with her son, arm-in-arm, along the most beautiful part of the Backs, where the trees are like ferns. He was wearing a gown and a white silk hood, and the college bells were ringing. Her eyes brightened with tears at the picture. And, because she couldn't describe it to him then and there, she leant forward and asked, smiling:

"How are you getting on with that book you've got to read, darling?"

The book was Pollard's *Factors in Modern History*. Eric had got it and several others to read during these holidays. Lily had looked into it a day or two before and had asked Eric to read some aloud to her. It helped his stammering. She couldn't follow very much of it—the author seemed always to be alluding to things she hadn't heard of. She began to realise that History meant different things to different people. She'd always thought she knew a good deal herself. There was a time when she could have told you how all the English kings were related and who they married and the names of most of their children. But Lily took a great pleasure in hearing Eric read the *Factors*, for it was all History, and how clever Eric must be to understand it.

When she addressed him now, he looked up, so

grave and preoccupied, with his ugly hands folded on one knee. It was easy to imagine him meditating in a study. He had been startled out of his thoughts.

"Oh, all r-right."

His answer was rather curt, very different from the way in which he usually spoke to her, but Lily did not notice it. Already she was back again in the past. She had almost forgotten him. They were passing the mill, with its rows of blank windows, high above them. And now they were at the canal and looking down into the lock, the water so black and deep down, and the tall weedy gates letting through no more than a trickle. Lily had come up here to sketch while she was engaged. It made a beautiful water-colour. The bar of the gates, black and white, standing out against the distant hills, and the barge coming down with scarlet hatches, and the slope of the ground spreading away from you—the woods just below and the church tower showing. That picture had been one of Richard's favourites. They had had it up in the dining-room of their little house in Earl's Court all the time they were married.

"I should think we'd better sit at the back, today," said Lily to Mr. Vernon. "It won't be so far for you to walk; and there's sure to be a crowd."

Mr. Vernon smiled, grunted, nodded.

But immediately it occurred to Lily: I should hate people not to see him. The Squire. Lily felt a tremendous loyalty to John as the Squire. He represented the Hall. There was a great deal of Socialism in the village, she had heard, since the War. Chapel Bridge had always had a tendency to Socialism. Lily had come to think of certain people as loyal to Papa and others as not loyal. Mr. Askew, who kept the paper-shop, was loyal. Mr. Hardwick, the bank manager, was loyal. Mr. Higham, the grocer, though polite to Papa's money, was not loyal. Lily remembered how good Mamma had always been to the people of Chapel Bridge, and it made her furious to think that these people or their children could repudiate the leadership of the Hall in the village life. But the fact was, the village was no longer a village, but a suburb. Rich men lived there, who went into business every day in quick trains to Manchester. Most of them had made money in the War. Lily could hate these people passionately.

But now they were stopping at the church. A great many people were standing round the door and in the churchyard. They were just going in.

"You let me get out first," she said to John, as she always did. As if she thought he might spring from the carriage and help her to alight.

Eric was out already. And now Mr. Hardwick, wearing a very high collar, was unctuously coming forward to give Mr. Vernon his arm.

"Good morning, sir. Good morning, Mrs. Richard." His tone was discreetly melancholy.

"One might say that this weather was quite ideal. Allow me. Thank you."

He was used to steering Mr. Vernon from the carriage to his seat in the bank office, where he was frequently informed tactfully of an overdraft; and the extraordinary violence with which John left the victoria did not break his wrist. Kent brushed some cigar ash from his master's coat, quite unaware that he was making the same noises as when he groomed the horse.

John shuffled up the path to the church door on Mr. Hardwick's arm. Lily and Eric followed. Several people raised their hats with discreet respect. Lily felt resigned to their sitting at the back now that she saw what a lot of people had come. If they didn't, they would never get out for the dedication at all.

There was Mr. Ramsbotham. Whatever was he doing here? Lily didn't know whether she felt pleased or not that Mr. Ramsbotham had seen them and was edging his way up. No, she was not pleased, she felt—looking at his ruddy, veined face, with its cropped moustache, hairy lobes to the ears and rather bald forehead. He jarred upon her mood, so neatly dressed in dark blue, with a black tie. And, as usual, he was wearing spats.

"Good morning, Mrs. Vernon. Good morning, sir. May I help you find a seat?"

He disregarded Mr. Hardwick completely; but Lily didn't, after all, dislike him. Evidently he knew how to behave. She had never seen him sobered down like this before. On that day he had shown them over the mill she had been shocked but rather intrigued by his naïve vulgarity. "Well, Mrs. Vernon, I'm afraid this is rather an awkward step up. I won't look, I promise." Or his gallantry, asking her to advise him about some samples of coloured string: "We always have to ask the ladies, you know, when it's a question of taste." And then, when he came over to see the Hall, there were his jokes about the "Leather Bottel." And of course he had discovered that embarrassing circular hole in the seat of the porter's chair, under the cushion. All the same, thinking of these things, she couldn't help smiling at him slightly.

In silence, with heavy scraping of footsteps on the stone, the crowd passed into the church, where the organ was booming. Mr. Ramsbotham had taken control of Papa. They moved into the first of the pitch-pine pews. The crowd in front was so thick that there was no glimpse to be had of the Bishop. The service was just going to begin.

Lily looked round for Mary and could not see her. Was it possible that Mary hadn't come? Surely not. But with Mary anything was possible. She was so casual. Lily felt herself turn cold and hard with resentment towards her sister-in-law. She hated Mary for the feeling that was coming over herself, at this moment, in this place, when she wanted to be pure and free from any thoughts except of Richard. Reminding herself of how she had felt scarcely half an hour ago, of her newly discovered calm and strength, she knelt down and closed her eyes. Her brain muttered words. In her heart she was praying: O God, make me happy. Let me be happy a little longer. But her brain did not know any prayer-words about happiness. It only repeated what it knew, tags about repentance, humility, goodness, mercy. Lily looked up towards God and saw the incredible blue roof of the chancel decorated with golden stars. And now the whole congregation was on its knees, repeating the correct version of the prayer she had imperfectly remembered. The mid-Victorian ugliness of the church, so gorgeous and solemn, with its ruby and emerald green and sapphire windows, bathroom marble tablets, scrollwork gas-brackets, check pavement and fancy organ-pipes, soothed Lily's mind. She felt a tenderness towards it, if only because Richard and she had laughed at it so often. She turned her eyes and saw Papa sitting bowed in prayer. He couldn't kneel. Eric's sleeves moved half-way to his elbows when he bent his arms. And why couldn't he tie his tie better? Her straightening had only made it worse. She would be sorry if Mary saw it. And this made her glad in a way that Mary wasn't there. But her heart was pure, now. She suddenly noticed Mr. Ramsbotham's striped cuffs.

They all rose to their feet for the hymn. For all

the saints. The draped flags showed against the altar for a moment down a long lane between the heads. Lily's voice sailed up. Who Thee by faith before the world confess'd. She sang beautifully, her eyes full of tears. Thou wast their Rock. Mr. Vernon's crazy tenor sounded in her ear. Mr. Ramsbotham was just audible. O blest communion! fellowship Divine! She couldn't hear Eric. She tried to see Richard's face before her in the air. The organ dwindled to *vox humana* for the Golden Evening. People round her were sobbing. Lily was in ecstasy. The last verse roared out in triumph. And it was their triumph—all theirs. They stood to attention while the Vicar read the names of the Fallen.

This part of the service had a strange effect upon Lily. The reading of the names, so crudely recorded, alphabetically, without any preface or title, seemed ugly and brutal to her. She had been similarly struck, though not so strongly, by a call-over she had heard on a Speech Day at Eric's school. It had seemed to her that this was a glimpse of the real man's world, so hard and formal and cold. She had hardly thought of Richard, as one had to think of him, of course, turned forth over there, on the Other Side, with Frank Prewitt, Harold Stanley Peck, George Henry Swindells—all so naked and lost, clinging together, learning the new rules and ways, dazed and unfamiliar.

"Ernest Trapp," read the Vicar.

"Richard John Vernon."

"Timothy Dennis Watts."

His name had sounded quite strange to her. She thought: I don't care—I don't see why it should be different from over here. Why couldn't they have read out the officers' names first? She'd heard that the names on the Memorial were put in the same way. That was really disgraceful, because, in fifty years' time, nobody would know who anybody was.

The organ began to play, and the choir sang "Onward, Christian Soldiers" as the congregation filed out into the churchyard for the dedication. Mary appeared at the door and touched Lily's elbow. They smiled faintly at each other. Anne was with Mary. And behind them was Edward Blake.

The Memorial Cross had been erected on the spur of land at the back of the church, overlooking the valley. The dark edge of the hill rose behind it, and everybody agreed that the site could not have been better chosen, although it was unfortunately not visible from the road. Kent, who had been waiting in the porch, came forward and gruffly whispered to Lily that the boy had brought up the wreath from Dobson's. Apparently it was hidden away in one of the sheds at the back of the vestry, where the sexton kept his wheelbarrow and spades. Was it to be brought now, or later?

Lily wondered what other people were doing. They must have made some arrangement. If the wreath was fetched out now, who would hold it during the dedication? They mustn't stand still either, or they would be left behind by the people on their way down to the Cross. On the impulse, Lily explained to Mr. Ramsbotham. He was unexpectedly helpful. He would go round with Kent and see about it at once; and then he would bring it to them, ready to be laid on the Cross. Lily thanked him with her eyes. Mr. Hardwick, not dashed by his earlier snub, appeared ready to give Papa his arm. People were very kind. Lily, emotional after the singing, felt a rush of kindness towards everybody, including Mary and Anne. In order to say something to her sister-in-law, for the pleasure of speaking to her, she asked where Maurice was.

"He couldn't come," said Mary.

Lily said "Oh," and smiled; for no particular reason, except that she wanted to show Mary that she was feeling quite differently towards her today. Perhaps they might see more of each other, Lily thought, impulsively. But Mary was so difficult to understand. She smiled too. But her smile was somehow baffling. To Lily she seemed always to be keeping her distance, rather ironically.

And there was Edward Blake. Well, of course, it was to be expected that he'd be there. Richard's great friend. And now Mary's friend. Lily had tried so hard, in the old days, to like him—for everything in any way connected with Richard must be likeable and nice—but she'd failed. Perhaps she'd just been jealous. That was natural. For he'd known Richard years and years longer than she had. Well, I needn't be jealous now, Lily thought. And he looked so tired and ill—no wonder, after the terrible things he'd been through in the War. After his flying accident, when for months, she'd heard, he'd been quite insane. Even now he'd a strange way of looking at you that was sometimes a little frightening. Lily felt glad that she hadn't to entertain him at the Hall. But poor Edward Blake, she told herself, forcing down her dislike of his presence, how terribly he must have suffered.

The Bishop and the choir came out of the vestry door and filed in procession amongst the gravestones towards the Cross. The orderly procession of surplices converged towards the dark straggling body of the congregation, from which detached themselves, forming into line, the ex-Service men, the buglers, the Boy Scout Troop. The order of the service must have been rehearsed, of course, but on the uneven, sloping ground the movements of the different parties were uncertain and tentative. They shuffled into their places, forming three sides of a rough square. It was very hot and still, and various everyday sounds—the crowing of cocks on a farm, the wail of a train in the valley—were disconcertingly prominent. Lily was unpleasantly aware of the nearness of all these people. Of the stuffy smell of their mourning and of their Sunday boots. Their grief, which had seemed beautiful and triumphant over death while they were inside the church, was now, under green trees, crude and hypocritical and sordid. Rooks flapped above them, scattering tiny twigs which fell from high aloft, spinning, to lodge on women's hats. People sniffed or cleared their throats. Some were coughing.

With an effort she withdrew her attention from these sounds and fixed it upon the Cross. She liked the design, and would have liked it a good deal better if there hadn't been so much ornamentation on the shaft. But it was in very good taste compared with the granite atrocities they were putting up in the neighbouring villages. She wondered what Richard would have thought of it.

Now they were all ready for the dedication to to begin. Lily and Mr. Vernon and Mary were standing almost directly in front of the Cross. Mr. Hardwick was on one side of Papa, Lily on the other. Mary was at Lily's elbow. Edward had withdrawn somewhere into the background.

Lily glanced round for Eric, and saw him standing just behind, with Anne. Anne is getting very pretty, Lily thought. Both Mary's children were good-looking—Maurice even more so than his sister. But I wouldn't change my darling Eric for either of them, Lily thought. And, after all, Anne isn't so pretty as she might be. There's something wrong with the way her forehead comes down. And her face is too broad. As for Maurice, I don't know.

There's something about him one doesn't quite like. He reminds one slightly of his father. But I mustn't go on like this, Lily thought. Why can't I be nicer to Mary and her children? Besides, I see them so seldom. How could I possibly judge?

And now the Bishop advanced with his pastoral staff towards the Cross. Lily crowded all these thoughts out of her consciousness, crammed them into a back drawer of her brain. She was humiliated and penitent that they should be with her at such a moment. She closed her eyes, fastening the eye of her brain upon a needle-point of concentration.

Richard, she thought, Richard.

And now the Bishop turned to the Cross, speaking the first words of the prayer:

"O Lord our God, whose only beloved Son did suffer for us the death upon the Cross, accept at our hands this symbol of His great Atonement, wherewith we commemorate the sacrifice which our brothers made: and grant that they who shall look upon it may ever be mindful of the price that is paid for their redemption: and may learn to live unto Him who died for them, Our Lord and Saviour."

Richard, she thought, Richard.

The Bishop's voice, so beautiful, so confident, with such precise modulations, rose and fell:

"To the Honour and Glory of God and in memory of our brothers who laid down their lives for us, we dedicate this Cross in the name of the

Father and of the Son and of the Holy Ghost. Amen."

Lily opened her eyes. She saw the Bishop, with his linen sleeves and the medals on his scarf. She saw the tall monument, the work of a good Manchester firm, tastefully executed and paid for by the large, easily afforded subscriptions of grateful business men. But Richard isn't here, she thought—she knew, with horror: Richard isn't anywhere. He's gone. He's dead.

Giddy on the mouth of a black pit, she faltered, scarcely conscious, swayed forward in an instant's nausea of pure despair, saved herself júst consciously from the fall.

A moment later she realised that she had caught hold of Mary's hand.

II

Mary was very much startled. She had been wondering whether she ought to have ordered some more of that New Zealand lamb. There was the week-end to think of. Not that any of them liked it so much as the other. And we really must economise over sugar, Mary decided. Nice-minded people had kept up their war-time habits, had ceased to want now what they couldn't get then. But the War hadn't cured Maurice of liking his three lumps a cup. As for saving, generally, it wasn't in her. She was snobbish about it. The idea of doing things stingily simply revolted her. Cooking in margarine, for instance, which most of their neighbours, who were much better off than they were, did as a matter of course. If you hadn't got the stuff—that was a different matter.

She returned to the service with a violent jerk.

"What's the matter?" she whispered to Lily. "Are you all right?"

Lily must have felt faint for a moment, but

she didn't show it now. In fact, she glanced up quite coldly at Mary and said: "Perfectly, thank you."

Mary couldn't help smiling. That was so exactly like Lily, to squeeze your hand one minute and snub you the next. But she really is extraordinary, Mary thought. I shall never be able to understand what she's driving at.

How strange it is, Mary reflected, to think of the days when I really hated her—almost as much as I hated Mother. The truth was, I merely wanted a scapegoat, and she was a stranger. It was easier to blame her than Dick. I suppose I was very unfair on her; not that it did her much harm. It wouldn't have kept her awake at nights.

The Bishop turned to address them from the steps of the Cross. He said:

"To-day we are gathered together at the foot of this Cross by a common sorrow and with a common purpose."

But no, Mary couldn't believe that she'd ever hated Lily. It was impossible. She still looked so idiotically young. There was scarcely a line in her face, although she couldn't be under thirty-seven. And yet she was frightfully cut up when Dick was killed. That was genuine enough. But it isn't crying that makes you look your age, thought Mary. It's having to buy the dinner every day of the year for eighteen years, wondering what everybody likes and usually guessing wrong, and then to bring it all home and cook it. Probably Lily had never cooked a meal in her life.

"There are some of us here to-day," said the Bishop, "who have looked on that scene of terrible desolation, who have seen, as I myself have seen, those shattered villages and streets, those blasted fields and those blackened trees. But to the others, those who have not seen that land, I should like to put this question: What did the War mean to you?"

Mary could answer that straight away. It meant filling in ration-cards, visiting the Hospital, getting up jumble sales for the Red Cross. It had meant coming up from London, because Father, after his stroke, had sent a message through Lily that he wanted her. It had meant leaving the little house in the mews. I'll go back there one day, Mary decided, if it's possible. Father, she knew, had wanted her to live at the Hall. And he'd have enjoyed having the children too. She was sure of that. But she couldn't. She wouldn't. Perhaps that was silly. Time changes everything. When Desmond left her, and Mother sent that message—how she got to hear of it was a mystery—that she could come back if she liked, Mary had torn the letter into little bits and burnt it alive in the stove. But it's no use being hectic. Mother was dead—and Mary was glad to hear of it; and yet it was painful for her to be glad. And when the War had come and she'd heard the last of Desmond and she knew that

Father would never get better, she was in two minds whether to accept. But this compromise had been wiser. She was sure of that, now. Lily and I couldn't have stayed in the same house together, Mary thought, for more than a week. I couldn't ever have lived in Chapel Bridge, and had Father looking in every morning on his way to the Bank.

And what had the War meant to Father? Dick being killed, of course. But he had never cared very much for Dick, she sometimes thought. No, the War hadn't been very much to Father, who could still, even when they were shelling Paris, take his drives, which got longer every year, up the Devil's Elbow, away over the moors towards Glossop, the brougham full of cigar smoke and the smell of the rug being scorched by Father's fusees, Kent cursing—back for warmed-up lunch at a quarter-past three. Tea with tea-cakes at half-past four. The evenings upstairs in the attic, reading endless novels by Guy Boothby, William le Queux, Phillips Oppenheim. Sometimes he'd sit for hours holding one of them, upside down, staring at it, breathing heavily. Yet they were soon finished. If you opened them afterwards you would be sure to find a wad of damp tobacco stuck between the pages. Father was what Kent called "a wet smoker." On these novels, on this tobacco, on cigars, on absurd and costly presents to his grand-children—he had once given Eric a mechanical swan which went round and round by clockwork in a tin basin—on huge tips, grocer's bills, losses through holes in his pockets, he almost incredibly managed to spend about two thousand a year. Thank goodness, thought Mary, I've got that money out of him for Maurice's school, whatever happens.

It was really hard on Father that he didn't see more of Maurice—his favourite grandchild. But it was so unpleasant bringing the children to the Hall. Not that Lily would make the faintest fuss, of course. Sometimes Father came over to lunch in Gatesley, and then Maurice entertained him the whole time, showing him card tricks, explaining how the dining-room clock worked, asking: "Grandad, what would you do if you were alone in a forest at night, and you had no matches, and no food?" balancing a cricket bat on his chin. But Father was getting too shaky for that now. She'd sent the children over to see him by themselves, but they hadn't enjoyed it much. They liked being on their own ground, especially Maurice. She didn't blame him. She'd got into the habit of seldom blaming Maurice, and this, no doubt, was bad. Maurice was altogether too charming. Again and again she saw Desmond, in the way he smiled, cut the bread, ran upstairs, described a conversation. It was like the explanation of a trick. She could watch her son and say, yes—it was that which attracted me to his father, and that and that. She could only be taken in once in a lifetime, but she could appreciate nature's cleverness. She could appreciate Maurice. This morning, for instance, she simply couldn't insist on his coming with them. And she might have known that Lily would notice—and remark on it. Well, let her notice. What had this service got to do with Maurice anyhow? No more than with Anne. But Anne took after her mother. She'll make some man a good wife, thought Mary, with resentment against men. I'll try to see that he isn't a Desmond, at any rate.

"I want to suggest to you," said the Bishop, "that this Cross stands for Freedom and for Remembrance. It stands also for Inspiration. I hope that, in days to come, the boys and girls who pass by this place will be told something of the heroism and self-sacrifice which it commemorates, and of the men who gave their lives in the service of that sacrifice."

There was one thing she would probably never tell either of the children. Desmond had spent his last leave in London. He had written to know if he might see her. They hadn't met for years. He didn't come to the house. He'd arranged a rendezvous by Cleopatra's Needle. He was forgetting his way about London now, he said. He'd been abroad most of the time. He wasn't changed in the least. They had tea at a Lyons' and walked up and down rather absurdly, like people waiting for a train.

He swore she was the only one he'd ever cared for. Where are the others now? thought Mary. And when this War is over, can we start again? Will you take me back? Yes, he asked that. She felt so much older than he was, old enough to be his mother. His mother, who'd written several times from Cork, very bitterly. She believed that Mary was the seducer, the betrayer of her son. He'd broken her heart. "No, darling," Mary told him—she shook her head, smiling, "I'd never have you back. Not if you paid me." She loved him better than ever at that moment, but differently. Love made her cunning. She would keep what she'd got—no more gambling. He was astonished, deeply injured innocent. He wasn't used to being treated like that by women. They parted quite good friends. And he was killed almost at once. She cried all day, but she wouldn't put on black. She wondered if the others had seen the name on the lists. It was never referred to. But perhaps Lily had gone through long indecisions wondering whether it would be proper for her to write and condole. Mary grinned. Lily was up at the Hall by then. She'd gone to live there almost as soon as the War broke out.

"There is one name, of all the names written here"—the Bishop made a backward, slight, somehow deprecatory gesture—"which I might specially recall to you. It is the name of a boy. Perhaps some of you here will, in a few years, be telling your sons: That boy was your own age when he died fighting that you might grow up in a safe happy home. Yes, that boy was not yet sixteen when he was killed at Ypres. I hope that his name will never be forgotten in this village."

Mary didn't know it, but thought vaguely that he must be one of the Pratts from School Green. She seemed to remember having heard at the time. Meanwhile she felt someone pushing through the crowd just behind her. It was Ramsbotham—Ram's B, as the children called him—carrying the wreath. He took his station just behind Lily. He was crimson in the face.

It was all extraordinarily comic. But Mary could hardly believe that Lily had ever given him the slightest encouragement. He'd been at the Flower Show and the Sunday School Sports—where she hadn't, after all, turned up—and at the sale of work. It was getting talked about. Higham had remarked to Mary only the other morning: "Mr. Ramsbotham takes a lot of interest in Chapel Bridge affairs."

And of course he went over to the Hall as often as he got a chance, which was about once a month at best, poor man. Why, she wouldn't wonder if he hadn't originally encouraged Gerald and Tommy to come over so often to Gatesley because he wrongly imagined that it was an easy step from that to being invited to the Hall itself. Poor old Ram's B.

And what did Lily think about it all? Did she

know? Surely. But Lily might be capable of knowing or not knowing anything. And if she were told she would probably be very incredulous, and then a little shocked, and then faintly, rather unkindly interested—as though she'd heard about some curious new disease. Yes, a woman of Lily's sort could be exceedingly cruel.

They all started to sing the first verse of "Abide with Me." Mary began to feel stiff, and realised that she was very bored with this service. Why couldn't they have had something much shorter? She wondered what the account of it would sound like in the local paper. She was quite sure that the hymns would have been "very sympathetically rendered." Would there be a list of the principal "floral tributes"? Poor Ram's B must be hating theirs. It was horribly awkward to carry, to avoid crushing the lilies or letting the moss moult or getting pricked by the wire. She daren't look at his face again.

And really, thought Mary, I suppose it's hateful even to think of laughing here, at this service, for a hundred and three quite decent little men who all got killed stopping Germans flying the two-headed eagle on the Conservative Club. Yes, I do feel that. No, I don't, she revolted. After all, that's only snobbery. All this cult of dead people is only snobbery. I'm afraid I believe that. So much so, that the attitude which we're all subscribing to at this moment seems to me not only false but, yes, actually wicked. Living people are better than dead ones. And we've got to get on with life.

The truth is, thought Mary, I want my lunch. And my corns ache dreadfully. And I despise men. Almost from the first, she knew, there'd been other women. Desmond scarcely concealed it after being detected once or twice. As he'd said, he had friends in London. Had she minded? She could scarcely remember. Yes, very much at the beginning. But soon she was used to it. She began to realise that she wasn't the only one who'd been treated in the same way. And there were the children. And the Chelsea people, whom she'd disliked and mistrusted so much at first, and who turned out to be quite decent and very kind. And there was her little house which she'd loved so dearly.

She'd often been sorry for Desmond, too. London didn't suit him. As an Irishman, he felt himself a kind of foreigner there. They'd talked of going to live in Paris, but nothing came of it. Ireland was out of the question. He could get no work, and there were his relations. His concerts, when he'd saved up for them—teaching, playing in theatre orchestras, and even once, as he'd foretold, in a restaurant, wearing a false moustache—weren't much of a success. The critics, he said, had made up their minds to ruin him. He shed tears. She comforted him. He was grateful, but soon went out; to be comforted more efficiently by somebody else.

Had Mother foreseen all that? She must have foreseen it. And how completely she'd been proved right. That was what I could never forgive her, Mary thought.

Nevertheless, she'd hardly been prepared for Desmond's note on top of the gas oven, one evening, just as she'd got back from a party. It must have been done quite on the impulse, like their elopement from Gatesley. He'd gone. Left London—gone abroad, as someone afterwards told her. The woman was an Austrian. They soon separated, Mary's informant said. Later, he'd come back, she heard, to London for a time. They didn't meet. He wrote, talking about divorce. She said that he must please himself. Did he want one? He never answered this—presumably because that particular reason for wanting one had fallen through.

It was a pity he'd felt that he must leave her. He had nothing to blame for it but his own conscience; and yet she had to admit that she'd been happier since. Even on that night, when she'd read his note and gone in to look at the children tucked up in their beds after she'd read it, she'd felt, yes, just for a second, in the middle of the awful shock, a little start of joy. Now I'm free. He'd left her everything. Why, he'd even left his old hat. And although, at first, life had been a nightmare that she'd have to write home and beg for money from Mother, she'd pulled round. She started the restaurant, and that had turned itself almost automatically into a gallery and a concert-room as well. And I'll start them all again, thought Mary—except the restaurant. I'm getting too old and lazy for that. The hymn ended at last.

The Bishop raised his hand, pronounced the benediction.

There was a pause. The buglers stepped forward. The Last Post blared out, setting echoes off among the trees. They blew like violent, ill-regulated toys—as if jerked by a strong spring. Mary thought of the cuckoo clock they used to have in the nursery when they were children, which always burst out of the door late—a few seconds after the hour. In the silence there was one explosive cough. A train whistled. Rooks cawed. A dog barked. A car went past along the road with a raucous screech. Nothing was silent except the black crowd. They waited for the Bishop to give the silence its end. To Mary's impatience, it seemed that he dawdled, as Richard had sometimes priggishly dawdled over nursery grace, knowing that she wanted to get down from the table. At last he turned. It was over.

They sang "God save our gracious King."

And now Lily took Father's arm and approached the Cross. Ramsbotham followed, awkwardly carrying the wreath. The Bishop, surrounded by the choir, had barely made his retreat from the scene.

It was a *coup d'état*, as Mary saw it. She heard

somebody murmur: "Old Mr. Vernon," and another, "t'old Squire." Lily had done the trick. She had produced Father at the service and vindicated his honour and the honour of the Hall before the village. She had asserted his claim to be chief mourner. Here he was. Nobody made any protest, although a voice audibly asked: "Who's t'old maan?" Father shuffled up to the step of the Cross. Lily turned to Ram's B, who handed her the wreath. She gave it to Father, and Mary thought he would promptly drop it. But no, he rose to the occasion. He managed to hook his fingers round the wreath for an instant, crushing the lilies, and advance one pace, before he half laid, half dropped it on the Cross before the tablet bearing his son's name. Then he stood still for a moment, facing the Cross, perhaps uncertain what to do next. It was understood that he was praying. Father's ponderousness had had its usual effect upon his audience. They were impressed. Mary, with a vaguely protective instinct, had followed the three of them out from the crowd. She was conscious of Eric and Anne just behind her. She didn't know whether she wanted to sink through the earth or merely to laugh. Then Father turned. She stood aside, anxious not to lead the procession. She took her place on his left, Lily on his right. Eric and Anne had executed a sort of flanking movement. They confronted the crowd, and Father looked up and slowly round from face to face as he lurched and shuffled forward. Mary felt rather than heard the admiring comments:

"Isn't he wonderful?"

"He must be a great age."

"Ee, look!"

"He can walk without a stick, and all!"

Mr. Hardwick came forward to receive them. The crowd opened to let them pass out to the carriage. Other people moved forward to lay their wreaths on the Cross.

Mary saw that Lily was radiant with triumph.

"The old gentleman was wonderful, wonderful!" Mr. Hardwick was telling her.

Mr. Askew, in a dickey and a sort of Eton collar worn under his coat, came forward and shouted in Mr. Vernon's ear:

"It's grand to see you about again, sir. It's quite like old times."

John grunted and said something like: "Awa ga ga, wa ga."

Mr. Askew beamed with pleasure:

"I was just telling your father that this is quite like the old times."

Ramsbotham had screwed his eyeglass back into his inflamed eye. Perhaps owing to some extraordinary scruple of delicacy, he hadn't worn it during the service. And he was so relieved, poor man, that it was all over.

"Can I give you a lift home?" he asked Mary. "I've got the car."

"You can, with pleasure. I was just wondering if we'd missed the bus. That is, on condition you stay to lunch. You'll probably meet your family."

I suppose I'm as near as Ram's B can hope to get to the Vernon family to-day, she thought—calculating whether they'd possibly got enough to eat in the house. Is there a reflected glamour about me? How thrilling. To-morrow night we'll have to keep going on cheese and salad, unless I send Maurice out to cadge a meal in the village. Which she'd done before now, successfully.

Mr. Vernon made further noises, Lily acting as interpreter:

"Ercurumber yerfther."

"Mr. Vernon says he can remember your father, Mr. Askew."

"Can you really, sir? Can you indeed?"

Lily turned from Mr. Askew to thank Ramsbotham for bringing them the wreath.

It's very interesting, thought Mary, to watch the tricks which a girl cultivates when she first comes out sticking to her when she's nearly middle-aged. Lily still opened her eyes very wide when she talked to men. (But no, thought Mary, that's spiteful.)

"I really don't know what we should have done if you hadn't been on the spot."

Ram's B was absolutely as red as a villa, blurting out about it being:

"A pleasure, Mrs. Vernon, I assure you."

"You must come and see us again soon."

Oh, there's no doubt about it, thought Mary, Lily is a little brute. That can't be mere stupidity. Or does she really like him? Good God.

What would Gerald say, and Tommy, to all this —if they knew? Gerald and Tommy, who probably prized their bachelor existence with their father in that tumble-down country house swallowed up in the outskirts of Stockport. There was no garden except a few grimy shrubs round the warehouses of the mill. No place to amuse themselves except the mill reservoir, on which they had a punt. What would they say to a stepmother and the end of their outings to Manchester—for one couldn't see Lily with them at the Midland, where Ram's B put up his eyeglass at every pair of legs in the room——? And their whole life—breakfast at lunch-time, Ram's B getting home from doing deals in Edinburgh or London overnight, having slept on the train, wrapped in newspapers, with a temper like a skinned snake, going out in pyjamas to have a row with a foreman, with a tea-cup full of whisky in his hand? What would she think of Gerald, who ran after every girl in the neighbourhood, though he was barely seventeen? They'd both got round their father to take them away from school. They told him some amazing yarn about their weak hearts. He was quite unable to deal with them. He yelled and cursed, and occasionally, when tight, would throw a bottle at their heads. Once they'd tied him to a chair—so they said—and left him to cool down. They seemed fond of him. Even Maurice had been slightly shocked at the way they stole money from his desk. They were hanging about the place all day long—except when they came to Gatesley—working in the mill when they felt like it—"learning the processes," according to custom, before becoming partners, but more often being hunted from one floor to another by exasperated overseers—rigging up machinery of all kinds in their private workshop, amusing themselves with revolver practice in their bedroom, trying to learn the saxophone or the mandolin, riding their huge motor-bikes all over the town and being summoned for speeding or not having silencers—ten times worse when Maurice was with them; the corrupton was mutual. The first Mrs. Ramsbotham had died years ago. Mary had heard that she was a quiet woman, refined and gentle, the daughter of a clergyman.

And now Mary had to talk to Mrs. Cooper and Miss Townend and Mrs. Higginbottom. They wanted her to help again this year with the Girls' School Outing.

"We thought of taking them by chara to Castleton to see the Caves," said Mrs Cooper.

Mary loathed the Caves. She once bumped her head nearly silly in the Peak Cavern. In the Speedwell Mine Maurice had dropped a new wristwatch Father had given him into the water. She said that Castleton would be splendid, and reflected that she needn't go in. Some of the smaller children were always frightened and had to be stopped with outside.

And then before long there'd be the teachers' picnic and then there'd be the Hockey Club Committee and the Whist Drives beginning, and soon they'd have to think of the Conservative Club dances, and so on to the Winter Sale of Work and the Turkey Fund bazaar, the Bethlehem Tableaux, the operatic show—probably *Ruddigore*—the School Christmas Tree, the Church Christmas Tree, and the performance of *As You Like It*. Oh, curse all this, thought Mary. I'd give anything to be back in London. But no, that wasn't quite sincere. The thought of all this activity and organising pleased her. She really looked forward to all of it—except, perhaps, the Whist Drives.

"I'm sure I don't know what we should do without you, Mrs. Scriven," said Miss Townend.

And Mary couldn't help being rather flattered and pleased, as she smiled at the little schoolmistressy woman in pince-nez.

After all, she thought—I do get some fun out of my life.

"There aren't many from Gatesley here this morning," said Mrs. Higginbottom.

"There'd have been more if they'd held it on a Sunday," said Mrs. Cooper.

Mary agreed. And suddenly it seemed strange

to her that Mrs. Cooper should be Milly Barlow of Stone Hall Farm. Milly, who'd been the witness of all those surreptitious visits—Mary pedalling over the hills on her bicycle in time to meet Desmond when he returned to Gatesley from his hated bank-clerkship in Manchester. Desmond was the Barlows' lodger. And they must, for many weeks, have been half expecting the tremendous and thrilling scandal which finally closed his stay. Does she remember the old days? Mary wondered. Of course, she must remember. Dozens of people in Gatesley must remember. How had she ever dared to come back and live in Gatesley, the scene of all her wickedness? To tell the truth, Mary had hardly given the matter a thought. She liked Gatesley—well, for sentimental reasons, perhaps, and when she decided not to live in Chapel Bridge itself she'd naturally chosen it. She'd had no idea of shocking anybody. If there was gossip, she was too thick-skinned to mind that now. She'd grown a thick skin during her married life. But an outside observer, Lily, for instance, couldn't be expected to see all that. It was quite likely that Lily had been very deeply shocked at Mary's callousness. Perhaps that was why she so seldom came to call on them. She didn't want to seem to condone the offence.

Mrs. Higginbottom said that she thought the service was beautiful.

"Oh, it was beautiful," agreed Mrs. Cooper. "I

think they did everything so"—she searched for a word—"so reverently. It was beautiful."

Yes, thought Mary—she must have forgiven me long ago. When was it, I wonder? When did I suddenly become respectable? Was it after the first time I organised the Red Cross Bazaar? Or simply when it got about that I was being received again at the Hall?

"We felt so sorry for poor Mrs. Richard," said Miss Townend.

And at last Mary was touched. The sincere, cinema-goer's romantic sentimentality of this dried-up spinster, moved by the sorrows of the beautiful and blue-blooded. There was beauty in the gloating of Miss Townend over Mrs. Richard.

And she made it better by adding:

"We were so glad old Mr. Vernon was able to get here, to-day. We were all so very much hoping that he would."

So, after all, Lily's instinct in that wreath business had been entirely right.

And now Ram's B was helping Father into the carriage, with the aid of Kent and Mr. Hardwick and Mr. Askew. Father was allowing himself to be particularly heavy, out of swank; like a baby being naughty and even sick because there are visitors. People coming out of the churchyard paused to admire the spectacle. There he sat, and they tucked him in with the carriage rug. The people gazed at him with curiosity. Mary considered her father through their eyes. He was among the best of his sort in these parts—where Rolls-Royce cars were often to be found in the garages of quite small villas. Landowners were becoming obsolete. Father was obsolete. The vehicle he sat in was obsolete. The animal which drew it was nearly obsolete—soon perhaps to become a Zoo exhibit or an outdoor pet. Perhaps he had a certain interest on that account. He would soon not be there. His present claim on their attention was chiefly that, by a sort of accident, he happened to be not yet dead.

Conscious that Mr. Askew and Mr. Hardwick—not to mention Mrs. Cooper, Miss Townend and Mrs. Higginbottom—vaguely expected it, Mary advanced to the carriage, mounted the step with one foot, and, leaning over, kissed John on the top of the head.

He submitted quite pathically, just uttering the usual grunt of acquiescence.

"How are you, Father?" she asked.

But he merely smiled, gave another brief grunt. He wouldn't tell her.

Stepping down from the carriage, she asked Lily, who was standing ready to get in:

"How do you think Father is?"

"Oh, wonderfully well, I think," said Lily.

And it seemed to Mary that she couldn't keep out of her voice just that slightly defiant note—as much as to say: Do you think I don't take care of him?

"He wants you to come over and have lunch with us one day next week," Lily added, heightening this effect.

And at this, Mary really couldn't help smiling. As if Father could possibly have "wanted" her to come over on a special day! That, of course, was Lily's way of interpreting Father's having said: "We never see Mary nowadays." And so Lily would have decided that it should be lunch. And on that morning she'd tell Kent to bring the Master home at one o'clock sharp. Well, and why not? Mary thought. What is there funny in all that? It made her smile, nevertheless.

"Which day would you like me to come?" she asked, and immediately wished she hadn't been so unkind, because Lily flushed and her face changed with vexation like a child that has been tripped up in some slight exaggeration by a pedantic grown-up person.

She answered, quite curtly:

"Oh, naturally, whichever day is best for you."

Poor Lily, thought Mary. Why am I so malicious? She remembered again how Lily had taken her hand in the middle of the service. It seemed that, after all, Lily was all candour and innocence.

Mary's smile became really friendly:

"I'll come on Monday," she said briskly, and kissed Lily, a thing she seldom did, as she got into the carriage. She could see that the public kiss melted Lily at once. They both looked round for Eric, for Kent was ready on the box. He was dawdling just inside the gate, talking to Anne, and Mary moved towards them, calling: "Come along, children." Anne was in no hurry, but Eric started and flushed when he saw that he was keeping the carriage waiting. He blundered forward, nearly colliding with his aunt. He paused for an instant to try to apologise, and Mary had the impulse to say:

"If you like to blow in this afternoon, we shall all be at home."

He looked at her with his large, rather startled brown eyes:

"Oh, t-thanks awfully, Aunt Mm—"

"If you've got nothing more amusing to do," she added hastily, smiling, to cut short that awful stammer. And she signalled to Ram's B, who was talking to Edward Blake, that they were ready to start.

III

RAMSBOTHAM was telling the not very new story of how, one week-end, the railway company had refused the responsibility of storing a consignment of his jute. So on Saturday evening he and Gerald and Tommy and a couple of watchmen had taken a lorry down to the station and brought the jute back, unloading it outside the mill gates and stacking it right across the roadway, so as to hold up the traffic. He'd been summoned, of course. Edward nodded, not listening to a word.

* * * * *

"I suppose everything'll go on much the same."

Richard had said that, the last time Edward had seen him alive. He was sitting on the edge of an overturned wheelbarrow, a derelict, minus its wheel. He puffed his pipe. It was a blue, mild day. High above Armentières an aeroplane caught the sun on its turning wing. There were heavy grumblings of artillery from the north. Behind them, some men were playing football near the farm with the hole in the roof—Richard's billet. They sat at the edge of the muddy road, watching an enormous procession of lorries slowly bumping forward over the pot-holes.

They had been talking of that unimaginable time, the end of the War. Unimaginable, at least, for Edward. He'd never for a moment, he now felt, expected to come through, to see it. And there was Richard sitting on the wheelbarrow, puffing his pipe, speaking with such calm certainty, as though he meant to live for ever. It had done Edward good. He came away from this last meeting, as from their first, reassured and soothed.

Their last meeting wasn't, after all, unlike their first. Then, also, the future had seemed obscure and uncertain. Then, also, had Edward been oppressed by a fatalistic sense of helplessness, of being a tiny part of a machine. Not such a big machine. Only a school of four hundred boys. Yet now Edward remembered more clearly than this later afternoon in France that dreary Midland evening. How they'd all crowded together—the "new youths"—mutely wretched, wishing to efface themselves, unhappily trying to avoid the questions, the sarcasms of their seniors. And Edward Blake had trembled, loathing it passionately, more than any of the others, loathing and resenting it. Hating his parents for having sent him to such a place. He'd run away, he told himself, at once. He'd drown himself. Starve himself to death.

He'd never submit, not if they tortured him. He almost hoped they'd try.

From the very first, he'd been defensively on the lookout for marks of injustice and tyranny. He hadn't long to wait. His fag-master gave him three strokes because the sausages weren't properly cooked. How could you be expected to cook sausages if you'd never learnt and if the study fire had to be fed with coal-dust? How could you be expected, after a single week, to remember all the idiotic nicknames of the various masters? And fancy having to clean boots. What an indignity. You might as well be a slave. How did people endure it? Why didn't they rebel?

Why didn't they rebel? he'd asked Vernon; and Vernon had answered vaguely that he didn't know. He supposed that everyone had to put up with it, at first.

Already they were friends, and took, as a matter of course, their Sunday walks together. Over the moist fields to the wood where people smoked or along the banks of the wide muddy river as far as the chain-ferry. Richard Vernon was barely an inch the taller of the two, but Edward thought of him as being exceptionally large for his age. His mild, good-tempered air invested his broad shoulders with an added strength and solidity. The second and third termers, in exercising their prerogative of bullying the new youths, had preferred to leave Vernon alone.

Of Edward, who was wiry and strong as a monkey, they felt no such timidity. They attacked him continually, in the passages, in the changing-room, in the dormitory—and when, fighting with the power of desperation, he managed to keep three or even four of them at bay, they merely doubled their numbers and, getting him helpless at last, applied their clumsy traditional tortures, mocking his tears, which were not of pain but of rage.

Richard Vernon seemed mildly amused by the difficulties which Edward was perpetually creating for himself. He did not altogether believe that they were so necessary or so unavoidable. But his sympathy was entirely practical. He helped Edward with his sausages, his boot-cleaning and his impositions. As for his own work, he appeared to get through it without effort. From time to time he made mistakes, was punished, justly or unjustly, like all the others. It did not worry him. He forgot a beating as soon as he could comfortably sit down again.

Edward was amazed by his equanimity. Impatient at and furious with it by turns. But he could never finally condemn it. He gave up trying to quarrel with Richard and surrendered to a deepening admiration.

Their friendship survived the passing of terms and the sharpening of the almost comic contrast between them. Edward was going to take life by storm. He admitted no final obstacle, no barriers. He could do anything. He would do everything. He was jealous of the whole world. All that he read, either of heroism or of success, he applied at once to himself. Could I do that? Of course. And, what's more, I will. At school, he appointed definite objects for his ambition. He'd get into the cricket eleven. He had. He'd get into the football team. He hadn't, but that was, partly at any rate, because he'd sprained his ankle. He'd get into the Upper Sixth. He'd only reached the Lower—having decided on the way that work was a waste of time and that all the masters were incompetent fools. Everywhere he saw a challenge. His schoolfellows delighted in baiting him, encouraging him to break bounds, to go to the Green Man for beer, to let loose a guinea-pig in form, to put a chamber-pot on the arch of the school bell. How well they had understood him. He dared not refuse. He dared refuse no adventure—horribly frightened as he often was. He would have fought any boy in the school, would have got himself expelled for any offence, rather than admit to being afraid.

He was never popular. His violent, ill-balanced temper kept people at a distance. His jokes, overstrained and malicious, seldom raised a laugh. He was accused of playing games selfishly. When he worked hard in form he was called a sweatpot; when he slacked, the masters wrote scathing reports. The little group of Sixth Form intellectuals might have welcomed him, but he openly spurned them. The rest of the House found him over-subtle. He had started his school career by hating the school; he ended by despising it. And throughout he had no close friend but Richard.

Everybody liked Vernon. As he grew older he was universally known as Uncle Dick. He played cricket adequately, was a useful full-back for the House, did a sufficient amount of work to satisfy, if not to please, his form master. His laziness, of which he now made no secret, was a perpetual joke. Unnecessary exertion he frankly avoided. While Edward never missed an afternoon's exercise—when games were not compulsory he played fives or went for runs—Richard preferred his study fire. The Spartan element in the House was inclined to be shocked, but, somehow, Vernon was never severely criticised. He had his own special position and it was respected.

Yet Richard, also, was curiously without intimate friends. He was taken too much for granted. People found him uniformly pleasant, but colourless and unexciting—a trifle dull. He never became involved in the little intrigues and antagonisms of House politics, and so appeared rather aloof. He was often appealed to, at the end of some heated discussion during which he had sat listening in placid silence, with an affectionate, faintly condescending tone: "Well, Uncle—and what do you think about it?" It was as if they were addressing an old favourite dog.

To Edward alone did Richard Vernon seem more than merely likeable. To Edward, Richard was a hero and a great man. In Richard's presence he felt genuine humility. Richard's strength and calm made him conscious of his own weakness. He envied his friend as he envied nobody else. Richard had no need to give proofs of his courage, to assert the strength of his will. He was sure of himself—therefore he did not have to fight and boast. He was brave—unnecessary for him to climb the chapel roof or swim the river in his clothes to win a shilling bet.

Never had Edward felt this more strongly than at the Hall, where he had often been invited to spend a week or two of the holidays. The Hall seemed the perfect background for Richard. The ordered quietness of the Vernons' life impressed Edward like a work of art. He was spellbound by the aged silence of the house, the garden and the woods. This, he felt, was the only place where he could have lived for ever, untormented by his restlessness and his ambitions.

And Mary, he had to admit, was all, or nearly all, that Richard's sister should be. It was only a pity that she'd been born a girl.

"But you'll be able to marry her, that's one thing"—had been a standard joke of Richard's, made always in Mary's presence.

Mary didn't seem embarrassed. She'd only laughed and said:

"Perhaps Edward won't have me."

How strange all that joking seemed now. Strange, almost prophetic. Well, it wasn't he who had deserted Mary, at any rate.

Edward hated to remember all that business. It had shaken, as nothing else could have shaken, his faith in Richard. It had come near to destroying it. He would never be able to understand how Richard could have behaved as he had. One could only dismiss it as pure cowardice—Richard's single act of cowardice—and blame Lily for everything.

And yet it was hard to blame Lily. Edward, when he first saw her, had been half dazzled, half amused. She was so absurdly pretty, she didn't seem quite real. And so childishly innocent. He remembered her one day at lunch saying that she'd read all Bernard Shaw's plays. "*All* of them?" some young man who was there had archly asked, thinking, evidently, that he was on rather daring ground. And, in an awkward silence, Lily had said quite seriously:

"Oh yes, the Unpleasant ones too. I think it's perfectly splendid of him to want to stop all those dreadful things. If I were a man, I should be proud to have written them."

Poor old Richard. He'd looked rather an ass trailing round after her, carrying her easel and paints. Edward hadn't been able, at first, to take

Richard's love seriously. It had seemed an essentially comic disease, like mumps. As for the fact that they'd presently get married and settle down and probably have a family—well, they simply couldn't. You can't have a family with a wax doll; not even the kind that opens its eyes very wide and says Papa and Mamma.

But the time passed like a dream; and soon they were preparing for the wedding. Nobody else, it seemed, regarded the affair as either monstrous or absurd. Except, perhaps, Mary. They never openly discussed Lily—they had too much loyalty for that—but sometimes their eyes met questioningly. They exchanged vague smiles of dismay.

Edward, of course, was best man. He had carried out his duties on the day in a mood of slightly hysterical humour. Richard, his tower of strength, had frankly and comically collapsed. He appealed helplessly for Edward's support, from the top of his hat, which had been brushed the wrong way, to the toes of his shoes, which hadn't been properly cleaned. Edward was duly reassuring. No, no, they wouldn't be late, they'd find his gloves, they'd got the ring. For several hours they were all transported into the world of the comic picture post card, they belonged to the genre of hired horses, bad eggs, curates, mothers-in-law and accidents to bathing-machines. And Edward, because he recognised this, had a sense of leadership and power over the whole party. His speech at the wedding breakfast was an enormous success. Funny, but in perfect taste.

* * * * *

And then, almost the next day it now seemed—although, of course, it must really have been months later, came this scarcely believable affair of Mary's. Unbelievable then as now, an accident without meaning, like something read in a newspaper. Of course, she must have been fond of him. But Richard's marriage, Edward could not help feeling, had had something to do with it as well.

A few weeks after the elopement he'd had a letter. She asked him to come and see her. They were alone together, and she'd cried when they met. Edward had never thought of Mary as being given to tears; it was the disappearance of one more familiar landmark in his changed world. For Mary was certainly changed. She seemed very determined and yet very submissive—ready, if necessary, to be defiant.

She wanted, naturally, to see Richard. And so Edward had gone almost direct from the untidy little house in Chelsea to the tidy little house in Earl's Court. From Mary closing the front door in an apron to a smart parlour-maid opening it in a cap. Richard, also, he'd seen alone. Edward had accepted his mission impulsively, sure of success. He expected Richard to be upset, of course; even, perhaps, conventionally shocked—as he himself had been—even, perhaps, angry. What he hadn't expected was Richard's shamefaced attitude of helplessness. For he didn't condemn. He was only very uncomfortable. He didn't, he said, see how he could visit Mary "behind the Mater's back." He was incredible and absurd—absurd as everything to do with the new Richard, absurd as his cosy little smoking-room with its washy pictures, absurd as his embroidered slippers. "Behind Lily's back, you mean," Edward had been startled by anger into replying.

But Richard, as ever, wouldn't be roused:

"It'd put her in a very difficult position."

Edward asked fiercely how, and was told that he didn't quite understand. "Perhaps later on," Richard mumbled, things would be "easier." This was too much:

"You seem to have forgotten that Mary's your sister."

That was the end of their interview. They parted —Edward furious, Richard pained and clumsily repeating that they "must meet again soon."

Mary had to be told—though Edward glossed over what he could. She was bitterly wounded he could see, but she took it calmly:

"Very well. Dick must do just as he likes. I shan't bother him again."

* * * * *

For a time, Edward had stayed on in London.

He continued to visit Mary and sometimes met Scriven, who lolled about the house when he was at home, fingering a cheap cigar. Scriven was half-guarded, half-insolent—taking it for granted that he'd be disapproved of. His handsome, sulky face drew into a sneer when he spoke. He asked a great many questions about Mr. and Mrs. Vernon, obviously for Edward's benefit—particularly about Mrs. Vernon, to whom he referred as "my esteemed mother-in-law." "If ever I make a penny-piece we shall have your whole family round here within the day," was one of his favourite comments. It was plain how Mary hated all this, but she wouldn't show it. She laughed and went on with her sewing or got up with some casual joke and strolled into the kitchen to prepare food. She was developing, under the stress of her married life, a quite unfamiliar vein of humour, adapted partly from Scriven's sarcasm, partly from Richard's rarely made, dry, mild jokes. She was building up her fortifications. Even when Edward and she were alone together now, she avoided the personal, warded off his tentative approaches and his unspoken sympathy with funny little stories about tradesmen's bills, people they'd met at parties, remarks she'd overheard at the green-grocer's, which baffled and finally rather bored him. He accepted her tactics and was funny, too. He could always, he now discovered, be funny. He wished he'd learnt the knack earlier, at school.

Edward had visited Richard, too. Even after that scene he couldn't stay away altogether. And both Richard and Lily had sent him notes—Lily's bright and semi-formal; Richard's cordial but brief. "You must try and find the time to look us up soon." That was irony indeed. Time—Edward had nothing but Time. He fidgeted about Town, dabbled and dawdled, could settle to nothing. From a seat in the park, from an armchair in his club, he regarded the enormous horizons which opened before his time, his money and his talents. Such horizons appalled him. He ordered a drink. Then another.

And at Earl's Court Lily welcomed him with conscientious brightness. She didn't like him, he knew that. Well, he didn't like her either. She left Richard and Edward alone together, after dinner, with some ceremony. "I know you've always such a lot to talk about." They had absolutely nothing. Richard, who wouldn't admit this, it seemed, even to himself, filled the silence between them with loud, uneasy joviality. When they were all three upstairs, later, in the drawing-room, the eyes of the married pair scarcely left each other for a moment. They appeared almost to forget his presence. Edward generally made an excuse to be out of the house before ten. At this they were genuinely surprised. Richard, indeed, had actually expressed his qualms:

"I'm afraid you find it pretty slow, spending

the evening here?" he had asked, with an anxiety which would have been rather pathetic were it not so irritating, as he stood in the hall, ready to show Edward out.

To escape from those two houses, he had travelled. China. South Africa. Brazil. Twice round the world. Had shot big game, climbed in the Alps, been round the coasts of Europe in a small sailing-boat. At any rate, he could afford to risk his life expensively. And he was happier away from England.

And then the War. And that last afternoon with Richard, sitting talking by the side of a muddy road. Edward was glad to be able to remember that afternoon. He'd taken a good deal of trouble to procure it, wangling things at the aerodrome, getting a fifty-kilometre lift, bribing the telephonist to put through a private message to Richard's mess. He hadn't expected anything but a sentimental pleasure from the meeting. And, after all, it had been a success. For Richard, away from Earl's Court and his office, had seemed again the Richard of their schooldays. He was busy knitting. He offered Edward a pair of mittens. And Edward had been wearing them when he crashed. They must have been cut off him at the hospital with his other clothes and thrown away or burnt. It was a pity, because he had nothing, absolutely nothing to remind him of Richard as he used to be, as he was when he died.

* * * * *

Ramsbotham had finished his story about the jute and was beginning another, also not new, about an accident with the transformer. Mary beckoned to them to make haste. Two men, said Ramsbotham, had been killed. Richard had been killed. Richard, who had said that everything would go on much the same. Richard is dead. And this is what remains, said Edward to himself, seeing the doll in her black, the slobbering old man, the gawky boy getting into the carriage. This is what we've got left of Richard.

IV

Eric jumped into the victoria, nearly treading on his mother's foot. Squatting down on the back seat, with his knees sticking out, he felt clumsy and huge—all bones.

His clumsiness was loathsome to him. He put his hands round his knees to make himself more compact in the narrow space. But his hands were as bony as his knee-joints, and always either too hot or too cold.

He looked at his mother, to see that he had not offended her. But Lily's eyes were fixed on the tree-tops, dreamily watching the rooks. He looked at his grandfather, and John smiled at him, widely, out of his bland, collapsed face. They were moving away from the church. The heavy line of Cobden rose above the trees. The white farms were sprinkled on its back like grains of salt. Eric began to think about the boy who had been killed in the War.

"I've asked Mary to come and lunch next Monday," said Lily to John. "Will that be all right?"

John smiled at her. Then he nodded, with a little grunt.

Eric had never heard of the boy before. He felt that he would like to find out about him, and wondered whom he should ask. Kent would probably know. Kent knew almost everybody in Chapel Bridge. When they were out driving people often touched their hats or nodded: Good morning, Mr. Kent, who never took any notice of Grandad at all. Mother said that this was simply deliberate Socialistic rudeness. But it couldn't be stopped. It wasn't Kent's fault.

That last spring of the War, in the Easter holidays, Maurice had said laughingly one day: "Suppose we join up, Eric?"

They had been alone together at the time, and though Maurice had laughed, he'd meant what he said, so Eric thought. Maurice had a way of half-jokingly suggesting doing a thing and then, if anyone agreed or dared him to do it, doing it at once—with so much decision that you felt he'd been meaning to, all the time. Only last spring, they'd been up in his bedroom one day and Gerald Ramsbotham had started talking about heights. Gerald said the bedroom was thirty feet from the ground. Maurice said: "No, not nearly that." Gerald said: "Anyhow, I bet you wouldn't like to jump out." "Do you," said Maurice, smiling. "How much?" Gerald said sixpence and Tommy said ninepence. Maurice had climbed out on to the sill and jumped. He landed in a flower-bed, the only one in the garden, and lay there shouting to them to chuck him down the money. His ankle was twisted a bit, but nothing serious.

Those words of Maurice's had thrown Eric into a fever of doubts and hesitations for the rest of the holidays. Almost every day he was on the point of going to Maurice and saying: "Come along. I'm ready." Every night he lay awake for hours thinking about it, screwing himself up. At night, in the darkness, he was brave. The adventure seemed possible, almost easy. He saw it before him in the blackness, lived through it in all its stages. They would have been passed, almost certainly. They were tall for their age at fifteen, and at that time, with the German Push going forward, they couldn't afford to be particular whom they took. Eric saw their life together in the training-camp, watched himself and Maurice drilling, being taught how to fight with bayonets, embarking on the troopship, cheering from French trains—Are we downhearted?—arriving in billets, going up along miles of communication trenches to the front line, waiting for the zero hour at dawn, in thin rain. He weighed, tasted every experience, every hardship—decided that, with Maurice, he could face them all.

It hadn't been a mere day-dream, either. Again and again he'd all but asked the question. And of course Maurice would have come. The truth was, he'd been held back by pure fear—nothing else. Yes, I'm a coward all right, Eric thought.

But suppose he had known then of someone else—of his own age—who'd done the same thing. This boy, for instance. That example might just have turned the balance. And so, one night, they'd have run away, caught an early morning train into Manchester, leaving notes in their bedrooms. And, as a matter of fact, the War would have been practically over before they got out to the Front at all. And now they'd be war heroes, old soldiers, as good as grown-up men, respected by everybody. Or their names might be written with his father's on the Cross. Eric preferred to think of that. No, not Maurice's name. His own, only. He had saved Maurice's life. They got him back to the base hospital, fatally wounded. He felt no pain. Maurice came and knelt by his bed. Oh, Eric, why did you do it? I don't deserve it. But Eric smiled and said: I'm glad I did it, Maurice. You mustn't cry like that. You must try to make things easier for my mother. Maurice was standing to-day beside Aunt Mary and Anne at the Cross. Maurice wore a black band round his arm. They talked of Eric. Maurice said: We shall never forget him. Never. What bloody trash, cried Eric to himself, pouncing suddenly upon the day-dream, kicking it savagely, smashing it to atoms.

Yet his eyes had filled with tears. As the carriage climbed the slope of the road to the canal bank, he felt all round him the heavy voluptuous sadness of the summer day brooding over the glittering hills. It was in his blood, in his stomach, in his brain; a cloudy, apprehensive sadness. Eric was going through a phase of nostalgia for his childhood. The present seemed mere chaos, cumbered with the inefficiency of his three-quarters grown body and half-developed intellect. He brooded over the shapes of the hills. He had discovered that they resemble breasts. Eric wrote poetry, mostly sonnets, in a small black book which he usually carried about with him, when at home, for fear his mother should find it. They were all about Nature.

One of his black socks had a hole in it; the roughness of his school trousers itched against the inside of his knee. He thought of school, where life was so difficult for him, so full of worries and anxieties, not to be late for work or games, not to leave his clothes lying about the changing-room, not to do any of the things which made people laugh at him. He got along all right if he gave his mind to it. He wasn't quite a figure of fun. But at the beginning of each new term he felt quite physically sick with worry. He would be glad when it was all over for good.

One day, thought Eric, I suppose I shall go to Cambridge. He knew nothing about Cambridge, but supposed it must be very different from school. Suddenly he had a brilliant idea. If I worked very hard there, I might become a don. He saw himself, an august, robed figure, lecturing: "And fifthly, gentlemen . . ." The thought pleased him. He grinned.

But I shall never be a don, he reflected, if I can't cure my stammer and learn to be tidier. The thought filled him with despair. But he made a resolution to himself. He would cure the stammering and he would be tidier. It was quite possible. Only he forgot. He was always mooning. At school, his friends helped him to overcome this tendency with occasional hard kicks on the bottom. "Mooning again," they reminded him kindly, without malice.

He could cure the stammering if he counted before speaking and always thought out beforehand exactly what he was going to say. And he would take trouble over his appearance and buy some brilliantine for his hair. But at that idea, a curious feeling of shame came over him. He didn't like to think of himself with his hair brushed and his tie carefully tied, wearing smart clothes. Maurice's hair was always as smooth as silk. But I'm ugly, thought Eric, with a certain fierceness. It's idiotic for me to make any sort of effort. I'm hideous.

And at this picture of himself, so ugly, clumsy, so inept at all the things in which he would have liked to excel—tennis, conjuring-tricks, juggling with oranges, doing stunts on a push-bike, ping-pong, card-games, understanding machinery—made only the more conspicuous in his failure by his stupid "cleverness" at History—at this picture Eric frowned with hatred and felt capable of doing something violent and dangerous, like riding Gerald's Indian all out, and not caring whether he got really seriously hurt.

His mother's eyes met his, and she smiled.

"Don't sit so hunched up, darling. You'll get round-shouldered."

She thinks I'm still a child, Eric thought. Darling Mother, she doesn't understand me in the very least. I suppose she'll always treat me as though I was still nine or ten.

He looked into Lily's eyes, so clear, so liquid. Their beauty filled him, as so often, with vague remorse. Darling Mother, I'm unfair to her. I'm always being unfair to her, and filthily selfish. I'm always forgetting what she must suffer. How awful life must be for her. I'll look after her always and make things as nice for her as I can.

This afternoon, Eric suddenly decided, I won't go over to Aunt Mary's. I'll stay at home. It was perfectly beastly of me even to think of going out to-day, just after this. I'll read to Mother or go for a walk with her. I'd much rather do that than go to Aunt Mary's, anyway. No, he couldn't pretend that to himself, not quite. I'm going to stay at home, at any rate, he decided. Eric began to form with his lips the word "shall"—shall we go for a walk this afternoon, Mums?

But he remembered that he must count before

speaking; and then, because that seemed too much trouble, he settled it that he would ask her later on, when they were alone.

Father had been killed while Eric was at school. This was his first year as a public school boy, and the telegram, with Mother's letter following it, had seemed merely to add the darkest tinge to an already melancholy life of war rations, fagging, loneliness, discomfort, strangeness.

Eric had respected his father, but had never been more than fond of him. Lily had claimed all his love, since the days when she had come into the nursery in her evening dress with spangles and picked him out of his cot before going out to a dinner-party. "Whose little boy are you? Are you Mummy's little boy? Are you?" Her kisses were rich with scent. And Father was only a figure in the doorway, a white boiled shirt-front surrounded by blackness, who said: "Good-night, old man. Darling, it's twenty past." Father was grave and kind. He took Eric out for walks when they came up to stay with Grandad, and told stories out of books in his careful solicitor's voice. The carriage was passing the lock gates now. Eric could remember just how the weather vane on the church tower above the trees had looked as Richard had begun to tell him about Sherlock Holmes. "Who was Sherlock Holmes, Daddy?" "Sherlock Holmes was a detective." "What's a detective, Daddy?" "If you'll listen, you'll hear."

Eric was very, very sorry to hear that his father had been killed. The news added poignantly to his sense of desolation in the midst of the great school. It sharpened the misery of hearing the ugly jangling morning bell, of washing in cold water, of jostling downstairs to work. It seemed that his father's death was in some way connected with the school. That the school was responsible for it, as it was responsible for the bell, the water and the work. The mornings were cold and raw, like reiterated sips of death. The dismal, untidy boot-room, the iron staircase, the bare dormitories, the stuffy little box of a study with the high weak electric light and thick blind which you got six for forgetting to draw—because of air-raids—and the soaked playing-fields and dusty class-rooms and icy-cold chapel—all seemed the atmosphere and scene of Death. For a week, Eric was almost intolerably unhappy, for a week only just less so, for a week still very miserable. Then he knew that he could bear it. It was no better, but he was stronger.

The days were lengthening. He wrote home three times a week, and his letters became more hopeful. They were full of comforting phrases. He almost sermonised to his mother, and indeed did actually repeat to her phrases from sermons in the school chapel about the War and the Fallen. He told her items of school news. And he felt sure that his consolations must be taking effect, because Lily's letters became shorter, less personal and more chatty. She in her turn told him news of Chapel Bridge affairs. The weather became beautiful. It was the end of the term. Father was dead. No longer, in Eric's mind, stood the stark word "killed." He was dead. Everyone told you that he was happy. Eric believed it. It seemed as though his father had never been alive, but was always, as now, an honourable, benign figure of legend. It made Eric cry sometimes to think of him, but only as music made him cry—a sad waltz. The idea of his father receded, became remote and sad.

He returned to Cheshire for the holidays, passing—as now—on his way up from Chapel Bridge station, the shop of the little Swiss watchmaker, and noticing that the window was smashed and boarded. The watchmaker had been suspected of pro-German sympathies, and now, so long after the outbreak of war, some rowdy munition operatives had made this an excuse for a "bit of fun" and nearly lynched him.

And when Eric had arrived at the Hall, excited with the pleasure of being home again and at the beautiful spring morning, Mrs. Beddoes had met him at the door, in silence, with only a wan smile. He was sent up to his mother in her room, as if to an invalid. He had come in, a little sobered, rather apprehensive, after knocking—utterly unprepared for the awful shock he was to receive. For a moment, he hardly recognised Lily. She was hideous with grief. Her eyes swollen into slits, her mouth heavy and pouting, her face blotched and sallow. He hung back, scared. The smile shrank from his lips. She gave a kind of hoarse cry. He rushed into her arms. That was agony. He knew then that everything he'd imagined he'd suffered at school was nothing, mere selfishness, triviality. She reopened the wound and tore it ten times wider. And now it would have made no difference to Eric if ten fathers had been killed. It was only for her he felt. Father was dead. But she was alive and suffering like this under his very eyes. He could do absolutely nothing. The words he tried to say were one long stammer. As for what he'd written in those letters, he was wretched with shame at his glibness, his heartlessness. He stood beside her while she sobbed. Suddenly she'd gasped out: "He loved us so much."

It was like a reproach, not for what he'd failed to feel for his father, but for all he might have been to her. He knelt beside her chair. An hour must have passed. It was time for lunch. He left her bathing her eyes with water from the bedroom jug.

This was the first and last scene of the kind they had had together. He guiltily shunned another. It would have been more than he could bear. When they were together they were gentle and sad, or sadly cheerful. Often Eric knew that she went upstairs to be alone with her sufferings, and on these occasions he went out by himself and roamed guiltily about the woods, torn between the feeling that he ought to be with her and the feeling that he couldn't bear to see her in that terrible condition. When he came into her room, sometimes, and found her crying over a diary or some old letters, he either stepped out quietly, or, if detected, pretended to notice nothing. Lily, on her side, never made any appeal for his sympathy, beyond showing, sometimes indirectly, sometimes frankly, that she wished to be alone.

Eric had been glad to get back to school at the end of that holiday. Even school was preferable to this haunted state, and the routine distracted his thoughts. The next holidays were not so bad. The load seemed eased a little. At times he fancied that she was brighter, but the relapses were more painful by contrast. They had never had a secret from each other before this. Eric had never consciously kept any fact or sensation of importance relating to himself from his mother. But now their whole relationship changed, and was likely to remain changed.

Nothing, it seemed, could re-establish it. Eric began a secret grieving over his mother. He was grieving over her now—over her paleness and sadness as she sat in slim black beside Grandad and the carriage rattled down the village street. Some of the shops were open, others closed, according as to whether their proprietors had been up at the church. If only I could do something to help her, Eric thought.

But he couldn't. And, what was worse, he was

getting quite shy with her, afraid of blundering—of giving her pain or offence. All through the service he had glanced anxiously at her to be sure that she could stand it. He was quite prepared for her to faint or collapse. He would far rather have had no memorial service and no memorial and his father forgotten, if she could forget too, and be happier.

And yet, here he was thinking about going to tea at Aunt Mary's. He had another pang of guilt at his selfishness. It was curious that the thought of Aunt Mary often made him feel guilty towards his mother, apparently without any reason.

He was still mooning when the victoria stopped at the park gates, and Kent began to climb down from the box, very stiffly and with loud coughs.

Lily had to remind Eric:

"The gates, darling," tapping him on the knee.

So he jumped out and opened them, as he had done since he was eight years old and loved doing it, after Sunday morning services, just reaching up to the latch, rooting the bolts out of the ground with a great effort, and always glancing apprehensively up at the notice: *Trespassers will be Prosecuted. By Order. John Vernon.* John Vernon would come slowly into focus again, as it were, as his grandfather—sitting mildly and blandly in the carriage

But some day, thought Eric, he will die. The idea did not greatly impress him. It seemed so remote. He could imagine his mother dying—it had been a nightmare of his for years. He saw her, so beautiful and young, struck down, killed by grief or quick consumption. That seemed sometimes horribly imminent. But Grandad never changed. Eric could barely remember him before his illness. He appeared to be immortal in senility. One would as soon expect a famous ruin, which trippers visit, to tumble down.

But when Grandad does die, mused Eric, pursuing this unfamiliar train of thought, the Hall will belong to me. That, too, seemed meaningless. Once or twice Lily had alluded in some way to the future, prefacing the remark with "One day, if anything were to happen to Grandad . . ." This sort of conversation made Eric ill at ease, and he cut it short with:

"Then you and I will live there together, won't we, Mums?"

"If you like, darling." Her smile was sweet. "If you want me to, then."

"Want you to?" He simply didn't understand. "Why on earth shouldn't I?"

"You might be thinking of getting married, you know."

"I shall never marry. I'd rather stay with you."

"Oh, but I should like you to marry. I should like to be a grandmother some day."

"Well, even if I did, it wouldn't make the slightest difference."

She had laughed. This had been one of her rare moments of gaiety; but he, who had been taking her more or less seriously, was faintly hurt.

By this time, Kent had touched his hat with his whip, said: "Thank you, Master Eric"—and Eric was back in the victoria again, having closed the gates. They were crossing the park, and every feature of that miniature sloping landscape was known to him. There were the woods beyond and the chimneys of the Hall just showing in the hollow. There were leaf shadows on the rutted drive. What should I do if all this belonged to me? Eric wondered. Perhaps I'd have the drive repaired. Should I change the name on the notice-board from John to Eric Vernon? But no, he didn't want to touch anything. He had grown up with a semi-superstitious fear, perhaps exaggerated from the teaching of his mother, of meddling with the Past. His mind switched back, as it always did, to her.

I'll stay with her always, he said to himself, and the thought made him feel curiously sad, so that tears filled his eyes.

Taking a sudden decision, he leant forward and asked:

"Shall we g-g——?"

"Take a deep breath and count, darling," said Lily.

Eric took a deep breath and counted up to twenty.

"Shall we g-go out for a walk after lunch, Mums?"

She smiled, so sweetly and sadly.

"If you'd like to, darling," she gave a little sigh, "and Mummy's not too tired."

She looked as fragile as a leaf. Again Eric reproached himself. She didn't want to, and it would tire her. But she'd probably come, all the same, just to please him. He ought never to have asked her to come. It was more of his lack of consideration. Of course, after that long service, she'd need a rest.

A voice spoke inside him:

If she doesn't come, you can go over to Aunt Mary's. He repressed it with an extraordinary sensation of guilt. In any case, he told himself, nothing would induce me to go to Aunt Mary's on a day like this. I oughtn't to. Out of repect for Father. Mother wouldn't like it. I ought to be by myself this afternoon and think about Father. It'd be disgusting to go to Aunt Mary's. She oughtn't to have asked me. But I expect she forgot, just for the moment. She'd probably think I was an absolute cad if I did go.

Edward Blake will be there, Eric reminded himself, searching for an idea which would make Aunt Mary's house seem less attractive. Eric hated Edward Blake. He was jealous of the excitement his arrival had caused the Scrivens. Maurice was particularly enthusiastic about him, because, it seemed, he'd done marvels in the War, in the Air Force. He'd got the D.S.O. and the Military Cross. He'd even been once recommended for the V.C. He'd shot down lots of German machines. He was a hero. And although he was really quite middle-aged and was going bald, with white hairs round the temples, he could do some extraordinary gymnastic tricks, like turning a somersault over the back of a chair or doing a standing jump across the table. But, quite apart from jealousy, Eric disliked him. Mistrusted him. He seemed to be sneering at everybody, and at Eric in particular, with his large, light-green, blood-shot eyes. Eric couldn't imagine how his father could have been such friends with Edward Blake.

And now they were at the house and there was another pair of gates to open. The figures of Mrs. Potts and Mrs. Beddoes were waiting in the porch, which meant that they were already late for lunch.

Since the beginning of the War, Grandad had had his meals in the room once known as the smoking-room. They only ate in the dining-room on Sundays. The room was too vast for three people, much less two, and, in Eric's mind, it was associated with visitors and enormous meals which went on for hours. Also, it had seemed vaguely patriotic to use the smaller room; as it had seemed patriotic then to do anything, however useless, which made you less comfortable.

But Eric liked the smoking-room. For one

thing, a convention had grown up that in that room you weren't expected to wait for Grandad to finish. It was part of the idea that the whole meal was a sort of picnic. Grandad would always wave to them with his heavy freckled hand not to wait for him while he finished his pudding. He usually had a second helping. Then there would be trouble with his false teeth. They tumbled out on to his plate. Mother always pretended she hadn't noticed. And Mrs. Potts would step forward with a napkin to wipe a large piece of stewed plum off his waistcoat, while Mrs. Beddoes looked up to the ceiling in serio-comic resignation. Grandad seemed to regard all this as a joke. He laughed quite frankly, and never made the least attempt to hide the mess.

Grandad might have saved himself a great deal of trouble if he hadn't come down to tea. Or if he hadn't gone up to his attic between tea and lunch. But this ritual of coming down to tea had perhaps been kept up in memory of Granny, who insisted on it. Eric could remember her saying: "Will you run up and tell your grandfather that we're waiting for him? We can't begin till he's here."

Eric had hated Granny. She was so sarcastic. It was all very well for Mother to tell him that she'd had such an "extraordinary interest in life." That only means that she was fearfully selfish, thought Eric, sternly.

Mother was very silent at lunch to-day. It

seemed more and more evident how tired she felt. Usually, she talked to Grandad a good deal and with great animation, as though she were a visitor. Eric had always admired this faculty of his mother's for making conversation. To him, it seemed positively wonderful. She was so full of interest in everything Grandad said, laughing eagerly at the jokes in his stories, which Eric hadn't thought so tremendously funny, even at first hearing.

Mrs. Beddoes brought in the pudding, and Eric was reminded of the days when, as a small boy, the lunch had come as a logical termination to the activities of the morning—when he had gone down to the kitchen soon after breakfast and followed the maids upstairs to watch them dust and sweep, teasing them, moving chiefly on all fours, so that he became familiar with the different kinds of mats, carpets and rugs in various parts of the house. At eleven, the maids returned to the kitchen to drink cocoa. Eric had stayed on there to see the lunch being cooked, had weighed out currants and raisins from the tin and had been allowed, sometimes, to grind mince-meat out of the machine. Finally, when lunch was ready and brought in, he would exchange glances with the housemaid, who waited at the sideboard, as much as to say: "Here's our pudding."

Granny had put a stop to all this. She disapproved of his going round with servants. It was all very well, but he had no one else to play with except occasional visitors, sons of neighbours, who drove over for tea, and whom he usually disliked—even if they didn't happen to dislike him. If only, thought Eric, the Scrivens had been living up here then.

Well, lunch was over now. Lily passed out of the room and up the staircase, walking slowly. She seemed deep in her thoughts.

Eric followed her. I won't say anything about a walk, he thought, if Mother doesn't. I won't bother her. She wants to rest, I expect.

She reached the door of her bedroom and, turning, said:

"Is there anything you want, darling? I'm going to lie down for a bit."

He blurted it out before he could stop himself:

"I only w-wanted to know if you w-wanted to go out this afternoon, t-that's all."

She hesitated, smiling:

"Well, darling; just as you like. But I do feel most awfully tired."

"Oh, n-no, of course not, then."

He turned very red. He felt every kind of cheat, deceiver. He was vile. He nearly insisted on her going, out of pure conscience. She kissed him, smiling. He turned from her awkwardly and walked slowly along the corridor, down the front staircase, out of the house.

The hot garden was very still. The stable clock

struck half-past two, with a sound which suggested a pebble dropping into deep water. Eric thought: I'm not going.

He walked slowly down the garden path to the door in the wall which opened into the stable-yard. But then, thought Eric, I'm really making a most terrific fuss about nothing. Mother doesn't want me this afternoon. Why shouldn't I go over there? It's ridiculous to think that Father would have minded. And at this decision he felt a sense of exquisite relief, although he knew he would have further qualms of conscience later on.

Eric could still remember vividly the time when the Scrivens came to live in Gatesley. Eric had barely heard of their existence before. He knew that he had an aunt and two cousins, but they were seldom referred to, and, of course, he had never seen them. Then one day Mother had said: "You'll soon be seeing your Aunt Mary." She didn't, even then, talk much about their coming. She answered his questions indirectly, but he knew instinctively that she was almost as deeply interested in the prospect of the meeting as he himself was. He knew, intuitively also, that his mother wasn't merely pleased at the idea. She was suspicious and tentatively antagonistic. He gathered that there might be something odd or reprehensible about his Aunt Mary, and that judgment would be reserved for the present.

He went down with Lily to look at the house on

Gatesley Brow they were to occupy—if Aunt Mary approved of it. She was coming up for a day or two to the Hall to make arrangements before bringing her goods and her family. It was strange to walk over that tiny, empty house and imagine his aunt and his new cousins living there. He speculated about them endlessly.

The day arrived, and he'd come into the drawing-room to find his mother sitting with a large dark woman, who wore her hair in circular plaits over the ears and was smoking a cigarette. His first impression of her was mixed. The cigarette and her clothes, which were somehow queer, over-sophisticated, almost foreign, repelled him. But her voice and her quick direct glance attracted him, seeming friendly. Aunt Mary looked a good deal older than Mother. She had a few white hairs already, some wrinkles round the eyes and in the forehead, and dark brown rings under the eyes—and yet, after a moment, one saw that she was in splendid health and full of energy. Her energy was of a quiet kind. She didn't fidget with her hands or talk quickly, but her eyes were bright and sparkling with life. She had kissed Eric in a sensible, friendly way, without making any personal remarks, and at once included him in their conversation, which was about her new home.

It had seemed queer to hear her say to Mother: Does Father do this, and Father seems rather that. Soon after she'd finished her cigarette, she rolled another one for herself, very neatly, taking the tobacco from a tiny red leather pouch. And this set the seal on her strangeness for Eric.

He'd kept glancing at his mother to see whether she was being similarly impressed, but of this he couldn't be sure. He had never been sure, from that day to this, what Mother really thought of Aunt Mary.

Eric passed out into the stable-yard, surrounded by the barns where a troop of horse was said to have been sheltered during the Civil War. Grass grew between the cobblestones, framed in the archway of the Clock Tower. Kent wasn't in the saddle-room. He must be having his dinner. Eric felt under the doorstep, where there was a hole, for the key. He opened the door, releasing the pungent smell of embrocation, the flavour of brasso and the mustiness of leather. He wheeled out his bicycle.

It was getting old, and had long been too small. He'd soon have to get another. Suppose he asked Mother for a motor-bike? Why, he could buy one out of the money he'd got in the Post Office. The absurdity of the thought made Eric smile. Not that he wanted a motor-bike—but Maurice had said the other day that he simply couldn't understand anyone having the money and not buying one. Maurice was always saving, but then he was always spending, too. And Eric knew that his cousins weren't well off.

For a long time he'd been very mistrustful of

them. They were strange, like their mother, but without, it seemed, her more reassuring qualities. Maurice especially, with his self-possession, his obvious sophistication, his pale handsome face, black hair and dark eyes that seemed wide open with politely unspoken surprise at the place they'd arrived at. They were at first frankly town children. They wondered what people did to get through the time in the country, and were anxious to be informed. They went about Gatesley and Chapel Bridge looking faintly puzzled, with the air that there must be more in all this than met the eye. Eric thought them supercilious. They had beautiful "party" manners. The first time they met Mother they made a very good impression. Later, she had seemed not to like them so much.

It wasn't till the Christmas holidays that the Scrivens had really begun to take their place in Gatesley life. It had been decided to have a variety entertainment in aid of the Red Cross Hospital, and Aunt Mary had been asked to help. After a week of rehearsals she was in command. She didn't push herself forward, but nobody could help recognising that here was someone who had a natural gift for managing things of this sort. The show was a tremendous success. Maurice and Anne had both appeared in it. Anne sang. Maurice recited a poem and danced a hornpipe. Eric had thought them absolutely wonderful—as good as any trained actors, easily.

He now expected that his cousins would become more distant, more supercilious than ever. He was quite wrong. They were so frankly pleased and excited at their triumph that he—and many of their other critics in Gatesley and Chapel Bridge—realised that they had, after all, only been shy and anxious for a chance to show their goodwill. After the theatricals, Eric began, in fact, the gradual process of falling in love collectively with the Scriven family.

For he was in love with them, it was nothing less. In Aunt Mary's house he was a different being. The presence of his cousins seemed to give him power. He felt wonderfully calm and sure of himself; everything seemed made easy and pleasant. He stammered less, he believed—especially when talking to Aunt Mary or Anne. He had been shy longer with Maurice, whom he admired so painfully, but at least he'd made no pretences. It would have been quite useless, anyway. Maurice knew him as he was—clumsy, bad at games without any sort of skill or elegance. Maurice knew that Eric couldn't throw properly, couldn't bowl overarm, could only swim breast-stroke, couldn't dive, could hardly have told you the names of six well-known cricketers, and was still completely in the dark, although he'd watched it and had the whole thing explained to him scores of times, about the proper adjustment of valve tappets and the engine timing. And the extraordinary thing was, Maurice didn't seem to despise him for all this in the least. They all knew Eric as he was. And they seemed to like him in spite of himself.

Eric still, however, had violent spasms of jealousy and self-disgust in which he saw, through all their kindness, a conspiracy to conceal from him that he was merely being tolerated and pitied. At such times he suspected their every word, every gesture; watched them narrowly and jealously; was even inclined to be curt and ill-tempered with them.

But Maurice, as if he knew of this jealousy, always turned its edge by making references, in front of Gerald and Tommy, to times when he and Eric had been together and the Ramsbothams had not been there. So that, if Gerald talked too much about the famous car they were building, in which they hoped to do a hundred, and which greatly interested Maurice, Maurice would nevertheless keep chipping in with: "You remember last Friday, Eric, when you said" so and so.

Indeed, he never seemed to resent the claims Eric's admiration made upon him. And if, as once or twice, his conversation about women with the Ramsbothams had really shocked Eric—not but what he was quite used to it at school—because it jarred upon his conception of his cousin, Maurice would notice this at once. When they were alone, he would be oddly apologetic, propitiatory; saying seriously and frankly such things as:

"Do you think I'm awful, Eric?"

"Do you get awfully bored with me?"

Remarks which Eric didn't know how to answer.

Once he'd been stung by jealousy to a violent, hypocritical outburst. Maurice had repeated an obscene limerick which genuinely amused him. Indeed, it had amused Eric. But it came from Gerald Ramsbotham. Eric, who'd had a rather humiliating afternoon, because they'd been playing cricket on the lawn and he was as clumsy as usual, suddenly lost all control of himself and broke out, in front of everybody, with something about being sick to death of all this filth. It was an almost incredible scene. Stammering cut him short. He had walked straight out of the garden and ridden off home, his eyes full of tears of rage, hearing Gerald's laughter behind him. When he grew calmer, he'd been appalled at his behaviour. Of course, he'd never be asked over to Gatesley again. He took that for granted.

But the very next day, when Eric had been sitting in deepest gloom, Mrs. Beddoes had come in to say that his cousin was downstairs in the hall and would like to speak to him. Eric had hardly been able to believe his own eyes. There was Maurice; he'd biked over, called on his own account, without being invited—a thing absolutely without precedent. And while Eric was beginning a preliminary stammer, wondering how on earth he could excuse himself, so hopeless of being able to do so that he nearly yelled: Get out of the house! instead, Maurice had begun saying how sorry he was about what happened yesterday, and he hoped Eric would forgive him—he hadn't meant to hurt Eric's feelings—he swore that he'd done it quite unintentionally—and so forth. And before Eric could get a word in edgeways, Maurice had ended up that if Eric had really quite forgiven them he must show it by coming to tea there that afternoon. Eric had looked hard at him to be sure that all this wasn't simply making fun of himself, but Maurice was perfectly serious. Obviously, though he didn't quite understand what all the fuss had been about, he'd made up his mind to placate Eric at any cost. And this had been all his own idea, as was shown by a chance remark of Aunt Mary's at tea that day. She hadn't known that Maurice had been over to the Hall. As for Eric—it was no use his saying anything now—he actually had to accept the position of being the injured party.

From this, and from many other incidents of lesser importance, Eric had learnt that there was a very feminine side to Maurice's nature. He was soft, like a girl. And yet this slim, delicate-looking boy would not only do things which the Ramsbothams would never have dared, but even made their very insensitive nerves tingle on his account. More than once Gerald had cried out involuntarily: "Steady on, Maurice!" They would take risks themselves, but he would do things which were purely mad—dancing about on the parapet of the mill roof, riding down the Brow backwards on his bike at top speed, or fooling about in a punt on the river and pretending that he was going to shoot the weir. He was wonderfully agile and erratically brilliant at tennis and cricket—but not at all physically strong. Eric could have put him on the ground without an effort. Sometimes he baited Billy Hawkes and the Ramsbothams until they lost their tempers with him and punished him soundly. On these occasions, after screams of agony, he merely laughed, showing neither resentment at their tortures nor the least shame at his own weakness.

Anne was not spectacular, like Maurice. She was quiet. She quietly fitted into the picture which Eric had formed for himself of the life of his cousins and his aunt in their little house—as the life of beings altogether singular, more gifted, happier than other people. It was this life of the Scrivens, as he saw it, that he had fallen in love with. He liked to imagine the three of them together in their home, at all times of the day—calling to each other from room to room, running up and down stairs, weaving, like shuttles, the strands of their existence, which seemed so mysterious to Eric because it was so happy.

The house was usually full of people. Aunt Mary would be holding a committee meeting in the sitting-room. In the dining-room there was often another committee meeting or a rehearsal, to which she would come and attend presently. Maurice's friends gathered in his bedroom or ran about the garden. Anne belonged to both worlds. She helped at the rehearsals, sometimes sat on the committees, lent a hand in the kitchen with whatever meal was preparing, mended socks, and then came running out to make up a four at tennis. The boys all liked her. She was admirable with Gerald and Tommy, who often kissed her in semi-serious horseplay: for she was handsome, though not exactly pretty. She was very dark, like her brother, with a bold forehead, too broad for a girl, and eyes drawn down at the corners, giving her at moments a wise, kindly, rather masculine appearance. But she didn't affect tomboyishness. She didn't wish or attempt to be taken on the same terms as one of themselves. The other day Billy Hawkes, moved by some impulse, had held a door open for her. She had walked through first, quite naturally, like a grown-up woman. It had given Eric a slight shock of recognition that they were all growing up. Anne had left school very young, because—as Eric had been told (they made no bones about it)—Aunt Mary couldn't afford to educate both her and Maurice in the proper style; and education was more important for a boy. Maurice went to a good public school, while Anne helped her mother with the house and Gatesley affairs.

This morning, in the churchyard, Anne had asked Eric to help them with the school picnic. Maurice was coming. They were to have charge of a special party. "And I want you to keep an eye on him," she had said. "You know what Maurice is. He mustn't take them climbing in the quarry."

So they trusted him. They treated him as one of themselves. They saw in Eric no fatal deficiency, no reason why he should not be regarded as normal, sane. Absurd as it was, he couldn't help dwelling on these assurances with the most exquisite pleasure. It seemed to him that, if he could live always with his cousins, he would expand like a flower, breaking out of his own clumsy identity, gaining strength and confidence. At that moment, at the thought of seeing them so soon, he was extraordinarily happy; he was transfigured with happiness. He stood on his pedals as he raced through the park. In less than five minutes he was in the village street, bouncing along over the setts, whistling piercingly. Several people stared. It occurred to Eric suddenly that he was recognised as the Squire's grandson, many people must know him by sight—and of course they were thinking it very strange that he should be racing about Chapel Bridge, whistling so loud, on a day like this. Perhaps they even know where I'm going to, he thought. He blushed violently, slowed down, then speeded up again, to escape them, up the steep side street, past the Sunday school, past the doctor's, past the Conservative Club.

But a moment later he had forgotten his self-consciousness. He was thinking that it would be well worth while to win an entrance scholarship to Cambridge, to work and become a don, if only to fulfil the opinion which Maurice and Anne had of him. For they had—or pretended to have, Eric added—a great respect for his cleverness. Maurice sighed at the mention of exams. "I wish I was you, Eric," he had said. And that afternoon Eric was full of confidence. He wouldn't fail them, if he had to work like a nigger. This, at least, he could do to be worthy of his cousins.

One afternoon, when he'd been riding over to see the Scrivens, Eric had had an idea which he'd later tried to put into a poem. Chapel Bridge and Gatesley were like the two poles of a magnet. Chapel Bridge—the blank asphalt and brick village, his village, clean, urban, dead—he called the negative pole. Gatesley—their village, lying so romantically in the narrow valley, its grey stone cottages surrounded by the sloping moors—that was the positive pole. And if you rode over from Chapel Bridge to Gatesley, from Gatesley back to Chapel Bridge, you were like a pin on a bit of metal filing, being drawn first by one pole, then by the other. That was where the poem had broken down, because a pin would never move between the poles at all, but fly to one and stick there. Also, "magnet" is an awkward-sounding word to get into a sonnet. Anyhow, Eric had the sensation, although he couldn't express it as well as he would have liked. As he climbed the hill to the waterworks he felt the strong negative pull of Chapel Bridge trying to drag him backwards like a harness. The Hall was behind it. His mother. All the morning's scruples. The War Memorial itself. But as he passed the waterworks, as he climbed the hill to Ridge top, the field strength of Chapel Bridge grew weaker. Weaker it grew, until the neutral point was reached, the farm which stood at the last corkscrew of the road. A few yards more, and the faint pull of Gatesley could already be felt. And now Aunt Mary and Maurice and Anne were drawing him forward, so that it seemed no effort to jump on to his bicycle and pedal up the last of the slope.

From the Ridge you could see right out across Cheshire—on a clear day, to the mountains. At night, the lights of Manchester, Stockport and Hyde were sprinkled over the north-western plain, seemed sometimes to quiver and move in the tremendous cataract of air pouring over the hills. And when there had been a snowfall, Kinder Scout looked awful and lonely with black outcrops of rock, under a bare sky. One year the Downfall had frozen to an enormous icicle, reflecting the red sun. Stone walls criss-crossed the wild, bleak country spreading towards Macclesfield Forest and the

Peak. Maurice had become an expert on ordnance maps, and though he seldom walked further than he could help, he reeled off, within a few months of coming to Gatesley, names which Eric had never heard, fascinating him: Hoo Moor, Flash, Stoop, Adder's Green. At the top of the Ridge it was always cool; though Cheshire lay trembling in haze. Eric got off his bicycle for a few moments, liking to stand there, feeling on one hand the lonely country of cart-roads, broken sign-posts, stone farms and walls, on the other the solemn wilderness of tram-lines and brick and the tall mills scribbling the sky with their smoke.

Then he sprang on to the saddle and rode on, past the quarry, where you could get white heather; past another farm; beginning to apply the brakes as the hill got steeper: suddenly turning a corner, Gatesley lay below him.

And now he was at the edge of Gatesley Brow. It dipped very steeply, trees arching across, the Buxton road running through the village at the bottom—so that, if you weren't careful, you got cut in half as you reached the foot of the Brow, by a car travelling at full speed.

In a minute I shall see them, he thought.

In a minute I shall see them, he repeated to himself, getting off his bicycle, standing still. He often teased himself thus, letting his pleasure at the coming meeting sharpen, by a few moments' delay, into absolute bliss.

He walked slowly downhill, wheeling his bicycle, until he came within a dozen paces of the gate of their house.

He could see the whole of the little garden, and they were all on the lawn. Gerald and Tommy Ramsbotham were there, and Edward Blake and Maurice and Anne. They were knocking a hockey ball about, not taking sides but tackling whoever had the ball. Edward Blake was in his shirt-sleeves and rather out of breath. Maurice, who loved, whenever possible, to dress up in some way or other, was wearing an extraordinary old straw hat, much too big for him, on the back of his head.

And now Aunt Mary had come out of the sitting-room, with Ramsbotham, through the French windows. She smoked and watched them, smiling, a bundle of papers in her hand. Edward Blake saluted her with his hockey-stick. Maurice, skipping about in the sunshine, got the ball and drove it with all his might into the fence at the back of the garden. His delighted scream of "Oh, God!" echoed down the Brow. Anne called out: "Idiot!"

They went over to examine the fence. Eric could hear Gerald Ramsbotham say: "Here's the ball, any road." Tommy, the more serious-minded of the brothers, went over to Mary and told her it was all right. "Only a loose board, Mrs. Scriven." Mary smiled and answered something. Then she turned and went into the house, followed by Ramsbotham. Maurice balanced the hockey-stick on his chin. Edward Blake came up behind him and tripped him with his stick. "Oh, would you," cried Maurice, "would you?" He tapped Edward Blake on the shins. They circled round each other, laughing and feinting blows. "Peace!" cried Maurice. "You swine, you started it. Peace! Ow!" Then Gerald and Tommy began a bully. In another moment, they were all playing again.

Eric turned and wheeled his bicycle slowly up the hill. They hadn't seen him. And now, he had the feeling that he had never meant to go into Aunt Mary's house that afternoon at all, but just, as he had done, to look in at them, to assure himself that they were there, as he had pictured them, on the lawn. He felt no jealousy now of Edward Blake, nor of Gerald, nor of Tommy. He was glad that they should have been there, helping to complete the scene. As though something were accomplished, he was ready to go back to the Hall. At tea-time he would see his mother, and be kinder and more considerate to her than he had ever been before.

And after all, he reflected, I'm certain to see Aunt Mary, at any rate, next Monday.

Free-wheeling down into Chapel Bridge, he was calm, almost happy, had even a certain faint sense of relief; surrendering himself altogether, now, to the attraction of the negative pole.

BOOK THREE

1925

I

"YES," said Gerald Ramsbotham, "to-morrow I'm going to get her flat out on the straight."

He lolled back nearly prone, his powerful thighs stuck forward like buttresses, clothed in aggressive check plus fours. His gold wrist-watch looked tiny and over-elegant on his beefy red wrist.

"The timing's all to pot," said Farncombe, knocking out his pipe on the fender.

"She's beastly stiff on the controls," said Moody.

"Did you ever know an American car that wasn't?" said Hughes.

Maurice looked down on them from the fender-rail on which he stood, twirling at the end of a wire what had once been the throttle-control of a motor bike.

"Teddy's Moon isn't," he said.

"That's a damn fine bus," said Farncombe earnestly. "My Christ, Gerald, you should see the way she picks up."

"I don't know why," said Hughes, "but I don't like Yankee cars."

Gerald Ramsbotham yawned and stretched himself:

"Did you see the new Brough on the corner by Trinity yesterday afternoon?"

"Yes," said Farncombe, "with the Webb forks."

"A Brough hasn't got Webb forks," said Hughes.

"The new ones have."

"Bet you they haven't."

"How much?"

"Nothing," said Hughes, yawning; "what's the time?"

Gerald looked at his gold watch. "A quarter to twelve."

"Goddy!" said Maurice, "I've got to see the Tutor at twelve."

"And I've got a lecture," said Farncombe, "unless I cut."

"You're going to give me that essay to copy, aren't you, lovey?" asked Maurice anxiously.

"It's in my digs, if you want it," said Farncombe briefly.

"Thanks most frightfully."

They rose slowly, yawning.

"What does Jimmy want to see you about?" asked Hughes.

"About Saturday." Maurice made a face.

"How much do you think he knows?"

"That's the point. I don't know."

"That girl may have said something."

"Not she. She'd lose her job."

"It must have been the old bitch, then."

"She didn't see us in the hen-house."

"No, but she saw the hen-house after we'd been in it."

"You were a madman," said Farncombe.

Maurice giggled. "They looked so damn funny with their little heads tied up."

"I don't suppose she thought so."

"Well, it didn't do them any harm."

"It did harm to the sitting-room, though."

"She's got to prove it," said Gerald.

"I'm afraid Jimmy won't want much proving," said Hughes. "He'll accept circumstantial evidence."

"There's no justice in this College," said Maurice.

"You thank your God there isn't, my boy. If there was justice, you'd have been sent down your first term."

Maurice giggled, flattered. Going across to the cupboard, he hooked his square and gown off the peg. His square had had all its stuffing long since removed. It hung floppy like a cap.

"Jimmy eats out of my hand," Maurice boasted. "Good-bye, you chaps. Don't go away. I'll be back soon."

All the same, he felt a little uncomfortable as he hurried downstairs and out into Silver Street—

not forgetting to put his head into his landlady's sitting-room and say: "Good morning, Mrs. Brown. How's the kitten?"—for it was most important to keep on the right side of Mrs. Brown, who'd even once or twice risked saying nothing about the times they came home from London in the early hours, without late leave. He wondered, hurrying towards his College, how much Jimmy really did know—and how much he'd believe. His thoughts ran on earlier rows. His first—his first term—when he'd let off that aerial torpedo under a Robert's feet on Guy Fawkes night. The Robert had been quite badly burnt and there'd been a terrific fuss. Maurice had had to go round and interview an important official, who'd ended by asking him to lunch. Then there was the smash-up last year on the Newmarket Road, when Stewart-Baines had been killed and they'd had to appear at the inquest. That was awful. Maurice had expected anything up to a manslaughter charge, but they'd got through it somehow, and only poor old George, who'd really had nothing to do with it, had been sent down. And then there were the minor rows. The row over the disturbance they'd made by bringing a boat with an outboard motor up the Backs and swamping punts. The row over the fire in Hughes' room after a birthday party. Endless rows about bills. Cambridge tradesmen were much too ready to get into touch with the College Tutor.

Thinking of bills was always unpleasant. He was in the hell of a mess over bills now. The people at the Garage wouldn't wait much longer. They were always the worst. The tailor was not serious. The gramophone shop he could square. God only knew what Mother would say to the Buttery bills. Anyhow, he couldn't expect any money from her this term. She'd been awfully decent already. Anne had long ago taken to flatly refusing loans. He'd had a lot from Farncombe and a lot more from Gerald Ramsbotham—but, after all, Gerald could afford it. All these sources were dry for the present.

I must wire to Edward Blake, Maurice thought, and ask him to come down for a few days. He'd written to Edward already, but Edward was hopeless. He never answered letters. And it was really essential that he should come at once. I'll wire to-day, now, on the way back from Jimmy's, Maurice decided. Edward might be able to help. Maurice avoided the word "pay" even in his own mind. It was unpleasant to think of cadging. But Edward had such a lot of money and such a casual, haphazard way of spending it—and the thought of money was like a nice warm fire. Maurice felt he wanted to be near it. It would be nice to see Edward.

Crossing the College Court, he mounted the staircase to Jimmy's room. Knocked. Jimmy's secretary opened the door. As usual, she was very bright.

"The Tutor won't be a moment now."

Maurice sat down with a faint sigh, wishing his gown wasn't so torn. Jimmy always kept you waiting. At last the secretary emerged from the inner room.

"Will you go in, please?"

Maurice knocked. Jimmy's voice sounded very gruff: "Come in."

And, of course, he was busy writing. So busy that he didn't condescend to look up at Maurice for nearly a minute.

"Sit down, won't you, Mr. Scriven?"

And Maurice sat, on the edge of the chair, waiting while Jimmy turned over some papers, blotted a sheet, signed three forms and finally took off his horn-rimmed spectacles and cleaned the lenses with a silk handkerchief. His eyes moved round the familiar book-shelves to the challenge-cup on the mantelpiece at which he'd so often blankly stared while Jimmy's mild sarcasms glanced around him and he waited patiently for the sentence—so many weeks' gating, so much to pay, or just a warning. His eyes unconsciously assumed that look of injured, yet not resentful, innocence with which he would presently be saying: "Yes, sir, I see. Thank you, sir. Good morning."

At length Jimmy was ready.

"Now, Mr. Scriven, I dare say you know why I sent for you. It's about this affair out at Huntingdon last Saturday."

"Yes, sir?" Maurice looked helpful.

"Well, I don't propose to go into a lot of details which may, or may not, have been exaggerated. I only want to say this: the Master and the Dean and I have discussed the whole affair, and we've come to the conclusion that this sort of thing can happen once too often—you understand me?"

"Yes, sir." This sounded bad, but Maurice was, at any rate, relieved that he hadn't got to do any more lying. He hadn't had an idea what to say.

"I needn't remind you of other occasions on which incidents of this sort have occurred." Jimmy smiled faintly for an instant, was immediately grave. "We won't bring up old scores. I only want to warn you"—Jimmy took off his glasses again—"that if any more charges are brought against you, substantiated or unsubstantiated, the Master will be obliged to send you down."

"Yes, sir, I quite understand."

"You will see that the damages are settled between you. I have talked to the lady concerned, and you can thank me that she will be satisfied with fifteen pounds."

"Yes, sir."

There was a long pause. Jimmy puffed squeakily at his pipe.

"Tell me, Maurice, why do you do this kind of thing?"

"I don't know, sir."

Jimmy rose, crossed slowly to the mantelpiece.

"I simply fail to understand it."

The clock ticked.

"Any sort of a damn fool can waste his time up here like that. But why do you?"

Maurice slightly shifted one foot.

"Do you know, your career at this college has been one of the biggest disappointments I've had in fifteen years?"

The clock ticked, incredibly loud.

"You could have been more to the life of this college than any other man of your year. I wonder if you'll ever realise that."

Maurice moved the other foot until the toes of his shoes were in line.

"And I'm not thinking only of the college. Have you ever considered what's going to happen to you when you leave this place? What sort of a position do you think you can make for yourself in the world? You can't simply bluff your way through life. That doesn't work."

"No, sir," said Maurice faintly. Jimmy knocked out his pipe.

"When you leave this place, you'll have to make a very big change. If you can. If you can."

"Yes, sir."

The clock ticked and ticked. Jimmy scratched the bowl of his pipe with a small sharp tool: "Very well. That's all I wanted to say."

Maurice did not rise too quickly to his feet:

"Thank you very much, sir, for helping us about the damages."

This visibly pleased Jimmy. He said:

"The best way you can thank me is to try and make this term a little different from your others."

"Yes, sir, I'll try."

Maurice hurried down the staircase, out across the Court. Well, he'd got off much better than he'd hoped. Jimmy was in a soft mood. The only snag was the fifteen quid. How in God's name was he to raise it? Gerald must be made to pay at least half—more than half—he could afford it. But even so—yes, certainly I must wire to Edward at once, thought Maurice. And it'll be worth it if I put "Reply prepaid." That'd be two bob. He'd only got a quid, which he didn't want to break into till this evening. But there was the college porter at the gate in his silk hat. Maurice headed for him.

"Oh, Brougham, darling, do lend me two bob till this evening."

"I'm afraid I've got nothing but a shilling on me, Mr. Scriven."

"Oh, well, that'll do beautifully," said Maurice, reflecting that after all he'd risk Edward's not having the energy to answer.

* * * * *

This term, the afternoon was always a bad time for Maurice. For eighteen months now, he hadn't been allowed by the doctor to play games. His heart was supposed to be strained by a motor-bike crash. He never noticed it. But it was a nuisance, because Gerald Ramsbotham played rugger, and Hughes and Moody squash, and Farncombe rowed; so that very often he was left between lunch and tea-time alone. Maurice hated being alone, even for a moment.

He paused outside the College Hall, wondering what to do. Occasionally, at this time of day, there crept into his mind, like a faint unpleasant smell, the thought of work. He'd done absolutely nothing now, since last summer. About twice a term there was a paper set, but it was easy to bring in a few cribs. As for his essays—that reminded him, he might go and fetch the essay from Farncombe's digs. No, he hated copying out essays when alone. It was much less trouble when one was a bit tight and the room full of people.

So he decided on the gramophone shop. It was nice to pass a dreary spring afternoon there, in one of the sound-proof cabinets, playing through dozens of records and buying one or two—they were very long-suffering. He was nearly certain to meet somebody there whom he knew. He knew half Cambridge.

* * * * *

By half-past four, Maurice's room was full of people. And Maurice came bursting in upon them in great spirits, waving a bag of cakes and the records he'd bought.

"Hul*lo*, you chaps!" he cried—his pale face puckering up into delighted smiles and flushing deeply, so that the veins stood out on his temples: "Hasn't the old bitch brought you any tea yet?"

He was so delighted to see them all that everybody brightened up at once, as they almost always did when Maurice appeared. They started the gramophone playing; and when the landlady came up with the tea, Maurice threw his arms round her neck:

"Darling Mrs. Brown, do you think we might have just one more little cup?"

"Oh, do let me go, Mr. Scriven, please; you'll make me drop everything!"

"Oh, Mrs. Brown, you are marvellous!"

At tea, Farncombe and one or two others talked rowing, football, actresses and machinery. Maurice, standing at his favourite position on the fender-rail, listened seriously for a minute or two at a time, seldom longer. Even when they were discussing the merits of the Scott Squirrel, he interrupted the conversation by starting a game of lobbing screwed-up balls of paper into the hideous new pink-veined marble lamp-bowl—Mrs. Brown's pride. And presently he picked up a golf ball from the mantelpiece and threw that. Everybody laughed at his gasp of relief when the bowl didn't break. Encouraged, Maurice took a glass paper-weight from his desk and, weighing it in his hand, holding his breath, lobbed it very gently into the bowl. It landed—but the bowl smashed to atoms. "Oh, Goddy!" screamed Maurice. And they collected the bits hastily before Mrs. Brown appeared.

"I thought I heard a noise, Mr. Scriven. I hope nothing's broken."

"You can't see anything broken—can you, Mrs. Brown?"

Mrs. Brown looked round, her every movement followed by the others, their faces writhing with half-controlled laughter. Actually, for a minute, she could find nothing. Then she realised:

"Oh, Mr. Scriven! that's too bad of you, really it is. My beautiful new shade!"

"I'm most dreadfully sorry, Mrs. Brown. I simply can't imagine how it happened. Perhaps one of its little chains wasn't very strong."

"And to think—I only bought it the day before yesterday!"

"I know, Mrs. Brown. It's most awfully sad. But you shall have another just exactly like it. We'll buy Mrs. Brown another, won't we, chaps? Has anyone got a quid?"

None of Maurice's regular friends responded, of course, but a second-year man named Currie, who didn't know Maurice well, eagerly produced it.

"Thanks most terrifically, ducky. I'll let you have it back first thing to-morrow."

"Oh, there's no hurry," said Currie, delighted to have been of service.

Mrs. Brown retired, partially soothed.

"That was a blasted silly thing to do," said Farncombe severely.

Maurice's spirits seemed rather dashed. He kept quiet for a minute or two. But conversation had hardly begun again, when the gramophone uttered a long continuous squealing scream. Maurice had been quietly tinkering about with it. The record was being played at several times the fastest normal speed. There was a general roar of laughter, in which Maurice delightedly joined. How he loved it when he could make everybody laugh.

* * * * *

During Hall, that evening, Maurice was in even higher spirits. He'd had a couple of gin and vermouths at the Buttery. The least drop of alcohol made him visibly excited. Sometimes, it seemed, he needed only to look at it. And in the Porter's Lodge he'd found a wire from Edward:

"Arriving lunch-time to-morrow."

That was splendid.

Sitting in his favourite place, commanding the whole room, craning his neck to catch the eyes of his special friends, waving to them, throwing bread at the College servants; scribbling notes, which were passed round from hand to hand, and getting back replies; fighting Hughes and Gerald Ramsbotham and being forced under the table; glancing every few moments quickly towards the dons to make sure that he wasn't being noticed—he got through the meal in his usual style.

"What shall we do this evening, honey?"

"I think I'll give the 'bus' an airing," said Gerald.

Maurice was pleased. He'd hoped Gerald would say that. He'd discovered, at tea, that their new friend Currie also had a car: a Sunbeam. He had pots of cash. And when Maurice had casually suggested that one day they might all go out together, he'd simply jumped at the idea. Maurice had asked him to coffee that evening.

"We'll get the others, won't we, lovey?"

"Sure thing," said Gerald.

Currie proved most amenable. After several more drinks, they went round to the garage to fetch the cars.

There were too few of them for Hide-and-Seek. They decided just to "crash around a bit." Maurice got into Currie's Sunbeam with Farncombe and Hughes. Gerald Ramsbotham had Moody with him.

"Where shall we go?" asked Gerald.

"There and back," said Maurice.

Off they went, flashing round the corner by the church, catching a glimpse of the Proctor and his Bullers coming up towards the Theatre—Maurice waved to him—past the station, out into the darkness.

The Sunbeam had guts, but it soon became obvious that Currie wasn't a very experienced driver. He was nervous when Gerald brought his car abreast and they raced down the road doing close on sixty. Maurice shouted and screamed with joy. Farncombe told him not to make such a filthy row:

"They'll think we're a girls' school coming home from a picnic."

They struck into side lanes, twisted and turned, until Currie said that he was quite lost. But Maurice and Gerald knew the way. They knew the country for miles round.

Swinging into a main road, they found an A.A. box. There was nobody there. Maurice had a key and wanted to ring up Jimmy. He would have done so if Farncombe and Hughes hadn't dragged him away.

"You're madder than usual to-night," said Hughes.

When, presently, they were passing through a long straggling village where there were still several people about, Maurice suddenly scrambled out over the windscreen, opened the bonnet and got hold of the accelerator control. He waggled it up and down. The car moved forward in a series of bounds. At the end of the village was a right-angle turn and a high arched bridge. When they reached it, Maurice opened the car full out. They skidded round the corner somehow and did a jump—it was a marvel how the back axle stood it—with Maurice clinging on like a monkey, his hair flying. Currie was scared, but he wouldn't stop the engine. He tried to take it all as a joke. It was Farncombe who shouted out:

"You damned little fool!"

Maurice climbed back into the car, temporarily subdued:

"You're not angry with me, are you, lovey?" he asked Currie.

"Do you imagine anyone'd waste their time," said Farncombe, "being angry with a little twirt like you?"

"Come and sit in the back," said Hughes, "where you'll be out of mischief."

So Maurice and Farncombe changed places. And presently Currie asked Farncombe if he'd like to drive. He was disappointed not to be sitting next to Maurice.

Soon Maurice had a new game. He fished an old plug out of his pocket and a coil of string. In another minute the plug was trailing out behind the car. They were leading. Maurice let out more and more string until the plug was bouncing along just in front of Gerald's headlights. Gerald put on a spurt, trying to overtake it. Maurice, screaming with laughter, sat on the hood playing the plug, which bounded along, skidding from one side of the road to the other. Suddenly Hughes yelled: "Look out!" A cyclist was passing. The plug whizzed out and caught the spokes of the cyclist's back wheel. Maurice let go of the string, but too late. The cyclist wobbled and nearly went under Gerald's car—for Gerald had no time or room to swerve. Finally he collapsed, cursing, into the ditch. Gerald switched off all his lights, and they vanished round the corner.

When Farncombe realised what had been happening, he asked Maurice whether he wanted to get them all hanged.

"But it was really your fault," he told Hughes, "for letting him do it."

Currie, however, had enjoyed the joke immensely.

"I've never laughed so much in my life," he told Maurice later.

At last they got to a place where there was an old two-armed signpost. The names on it were quite illegible.

"That's not much good to anybody," said Hughes.

"Let's take it back with us," said Maurice.

Amidst roars of laughter, they dug with spanners in the earth, straining now and then at the post. By combined efforts they worked it loose.

"I'm afraid it'll dirty your lovely clean car," said Maurice.

"That doesn't matter a bit," said Currie, who was feeling a tremendous devil.

On the way back to Cambridge, they discussed where it should be put. Maurice's digs was the only possible place. They'd haul it up through the window. It was late. There weren't many people about. Maurice held its head, Farncombe its middle and Hughes its foot. It was wrapped in rugs.

They only met one person—an undergraduate—on the way from the car to the door. As he passed them, Maurice exclaimed:

"Hul*lo*, Eric! Where have you sprung from? I never see you nowadays."

Eric, faintly smiling, very sober, said:

"I've been out to dinner with a don."

"How lovely!" Maurice laughed. "Well, look, darling, when am I going to see you?"

Maurice didn't quite know why he said it. But he never could help giving invitations:

"Look here; come to lunch to-morrow."

Eric seemed about to make some objection.

"You *must*, see?"

Eric smiled: "Very well. Thank you."

"That's glorious. At half-past one. Edward Blake's going to be there."

They were silent. Eric said:

"What's this you've got?"

Maurice raised a corner of the rug.

"It's the Unknown Warrior. Don't tell the Vice-Chancellor, will you, lovey?"

"No, I won't. Good night."

"Was that your cousin?" Farncombe asked, when Eric had gone.

"Yes."

"He isn't very like you, is he?"

"No," said Maurice, "worse luck. He's the brainiest man in Cambridge."

II

My God, thought Eric, at the window of his large, dark, bare room, looking down into the College Court, where the Tutor was just emerging from a doorway in earnest conversation with the Dean, who wore shorts, dressed for fives; three young men with gowns slung over their shoulders were grouped chatting; a College servant hurried, carrying a pair of boots—how I hate them all!

Standing there, he enclosed, he enfolded them all in his hatred—the discreet funny dons, telling legends about Proust; the sincere young neurotics, writing each other ten-page notes explaining their conduct at a last night's tiff; the hearties, divided between shop-girls, poker and the C.U.I.C.C.U.; the College servants, so oily in their deference to all these rich young ninnies; the bed-makers, thievish gossipy old hags, who drank as much of their gentlemen's whisky as they dared, and stank so that you could hardly put your nose inside their broom-cupboards after they had gone. And if, at that moment, Eric could have given the order, the

Round Church and the Hall of Trinity and King's Chapel and Corpus Library and dozens of other world-famed architectural lumber-rooms of priceless venerable rubbish would have gone up sky-high with enormous charges of dynamite, and the silk-jumpered young gentlemen and dear old professors been driven out of their well-furnished academic hotels at the point of the bayonet. And Cambridge would have returned to its proper status as a small market-town, inhabited by commercial travellers, auctioneers, cattle-dealers, out-of-work jockeys, and other bar-flies—a soured, defeated tribe, given over to betting and drink, in the middle of this swamp of a country, with rheumatics and damaged lungs. And good riddance, Eric thought.

Well, anyhow, whether I go or not—he knows what I think, Eric reflected. He'd been pretty frank in London last Vac. And Maurice had actually seemed impressed. Yes, Eric, I quite understand. No, I think you're absolutely right. Thanks awfully for telling me.

From anybody else it'd be a deliberate insult. But Maurice never insulted anybody in his life. He couldn't. He was merely being, as usual, quite thoughtless, like a child.

And how sick I am of children, Eric thought. Everybody up here is a child—a nice, jolly, overgrown boy. All of them artless and kittenish and naïve. Maurice does it better than the others. He's more genuine. But I'm sick of the whole push.

Altogether, that visit to London last Vac. had been a most miserable failure. Eric had looked forward to it all through last term. It was to be an escape from Chapel Bridge, from the whole situation at the Hall. He was going to get back into the old Gatesley atmosphere.

He didn't. Aunt Mary's house in the mews seemed to have nothing whatever in common with her other home. And even the Ramsbothams, even Billy Hawkes, seemed preferable to Aunt Mary's new strident friends in their large black hats. Aunt Mary was the same, of course. And so was Anne. But they spoke a new language. They seemed less remarkable; less unique. They had lost power.

Only Maurice, Eric felt, hadn't become, as he put it to himself, a Londoner. Maurice had not suffered from transplantation. And that was why it had seemed worth while saying what he had. He'd been careful, of course, to mention no names. But surely not even Maurice could be so dense—no, there was no way round it, Maurice must have known exactly whom Eric meant.

And here was all the result—an invitation to lunch.

* * * * *

Eric hated the Hall. Sometimes he felt positively suffocated there, as though he'd choke.

"When it's mine," he told Lily, "I shall have it pulled down."

She was not horrified, for she didn't really believe him. Seeing this, he launched into Communistic schemes, quoted Lenin, talked priggishly of the Manchester slums:

"We've no right to live here when all these people are starving."

But she wouldn't argue. He had to go on goading her:

"I know what I shall do. I shall give the land to the Corporation for a model village."

She replied:

"I don't know what I should do if anything happened to the Hall."

She was not attending to what he said, aware only of the tone of his voice and its intention of wounding her. Her listless sadness made him suddenly fierce.

"You care more for this house than you do for human beings."

She only answered, obstinately sad:

"I care for it because it reminds me of the time when I was happy."

And there they were, together in the slowly decaying house, alone to all intents and purposes, for Grandad was now so comatose that you could hardly describe him as alive at all, and Mrs. Potts and Mrs. Beddoes kept their respectful distance—alone, with no Gatesley, no Scrivens, slowly grinding down each other's nerves.

In lucid intervals he even discussed the situation

with her, trying to rationalise, be clinical. He'd glibly generalised: "It's the same with everyone. Parents never get on well with their children. That's just human nature." Had they both at the same instant remembered Aunt Mary? But Lily only sat with moist eyes and shook her head:

"All this is very difficult for me to understand. I don't think my generation felt these things."

"But, Mother, you must see that this can't go on. What are we to do?"

"Darling, you know I only want you to be happy. You must do whatever you think best."

No, she wouldn't help. She surrendered nothing.

But neither do I, Eric admitted to himself.

"You're always arguing," she told him once.

"I hate arguing."

Her gentle, ironic smile. He'd burst out ludicrously:

"I hate arguing, because I'm always in the right."

It was horrible. It became a habit. There was barely a subject they could safely mention. And always, as it seemed to him later, the fault was entirely his. He was crude, overbearing. She was mild and persistent. She seemed barely to argue at all—merely, with an air of distaste, she kept the discussion alive. And in his stammering days, when he'd first begun to lecture her, she'd waited patiently for him while he gasped and mouthed—red with fury at his own impediment.

But he'd suffered enough in exchange. His self-reproaches tortured him. His diary was full of vows that he'd be better, that this miserable bickering should stop. He wildly exaggerated trifles. "Another *vile* scene this morning," was an entry which recurred. He'd said to himself: What would Father have thought? Father, who'd left her in his charge. Suppose Father were to come back from the grave, suppose it turned out that he'd never been killed, was a shell-shock case, unidentified, in a far-away hospital—and suddenly his memory returned? This was one of Eric's nightmares. Father would come back to find that the two people he loved, who'd once loved each other so much, were leading this sordid, miserable life. Eric thought: But I should shoot myself or die of shame.

And yet this existence continued, did not improve. A horrible facility grew upon them, so that they acquiesced in it. And now it had begun to dawn upon Eric that the suffering was not equally shared. His mother, he now knew, did not feel this friction as he did. Often she'd seem even unaware that what he'd later describe as a "*vile* scene" was taking place. He detected, with sorrow, a certain hardening and blunting of her sensibilities. She could give a sharp answer without realising that she was quarrelling. And this, a reflection of himself in her, gave him more pain than any other aspect of their relationship.

There had been really serious quarrels, of course. Quarrels leaving half-healed wounds which were daily reopened by sarcasms, trivialities.

One day he'd come in tired and found a strange book lying in his bedroom—*Mrs. Eddy*. He was in an absurd, resentful mood. He remembered a friend of his mother's whom he disliked, a Miss Prendergast. She lived in the village. All at once he'd seen a vile, a loathsome plot to do a little stealthy propaganda. He'd stalked in to confront his mother:

"How did this book get into my room?"

"What book, darling?"

"This." He tossed it down on the sofa beside her.

She was annoyed at his rudeness. She answered more coldly:

"I suppose I must have left it there by mistake."

"Is it yours?"

"It belongs to Miss Prendergast."

"Then I wish she'd keep it."

"She lent it to me to read," said Lily. "It's very interesting."

Eric burst out in a tone of ferocious mockery:

"I thought you were such a great Protestant."

"That doesn't prevent me from listening to what other people have to say."

"You think people ought to dabble in every Religion?"

"I think people ought to be broad-minded."

"You Protestants aren't very broad-minded about Rome."

" 'You Protestants,' " she couldn't help smiling at this; "why, what are you, darling?"

"It doesn't matter what I am. I'm an ath——" but he couldn't pronounce the ridiculous word. Turning furiously, he made a violent gesture: "I don't believe in anything."

She took it quite seriously, rather disconcerting him, for he was prepared to meet a sneer.

She answered:

"But surely you don't object to different people seeing the Truth in different ways?"

"You don't understand. I do object. Because it isn't the Truth. I don't just tolerate Religion; I loathe it. All Religion is vile. And religious people are all either hypocrites or idiots."

There! He'd said it, at last. But she only answered with chilly dignity:

"If you feel like that, I can't imagine why you come to church with me on Sundays."

"I come to keep you company," he said. "In future I won't—if you'd rather not."

"I'd much rather you stayed at home."

That was the end of that interview. Later in the evening he'd come in and found her in tears. They had had a reconciliation. He begged forgiveness for his rudeness. They kissed each other. In bed that night, and during the next day, Eric thought over what he had said. And although he was full of compunction for his treatment of her, and the thought of that quarrel was almost intolerable to him, he couldn't, nevertheless, take back, in his own mind, anything he'd said about Religion. It seemed to him that he had only expressed what had been his conviction for a long time. When next Sunday came round he was prepared, all the same, to go with his mother to church if she asked him to do so. He was sufficiently eager for a complete reconciliation. But Lily didn't ask him. She never asked him again.

* * * * *

Eric turned away from the window, deeply sighed. He was weary—weary to the bone. He was weary of the Hall, of Cambridge, of London, of himself, of everything and everybody. He was too tired to feel unhappy, except by starts. And now he'd got to work. He was always working. He was getting very round-shouldered and his head continually ached. He needed stronger glasses. He knew it and did nothing. There was a certain satisfaction in doing injury to his health and a certain pride in his obstinate, stupid powers of resistance. Other people had nervous breakdowns. He despised them. He knew that, tired out as he was, he'd get through the Trip. He'd get a first. Other people were brilliant and erratic. He just slogged on. He couldn't help it. If he'd gone into the examination-room with the deliberate intention of failing, he couldn't have brought himself to it—his nature would have revolted. His Tutor had no need to urge him anxiously, as he sometimes did: "Don't overstrain. Don't get stale." He wasn't a neurotic heavy-weight boxer. He wouldn't disappoint his backers.

In his first year, Eric had been something of a social success. To be a senior scholar was, after all, a distinction. And for a time he'd lent himself to the atmosphere, gone in for politics, written articles in one of the less frivolous University magazines, occasionally even spoken at the Union, where his measured sentences, carefully avoiding the stammer, had produced an impression. He'd joined a running club and gone for long gruelling runs. Now all that seemed mere waste of time. He'd dropped completely out of College life, become a recluse, the subject of mild jokes.

After all, Eric decided, I'll go. What do I care if he's there or not. It'll make a change. I shall get out of this room for an hour or two, at any rate.

But now I must work, thought Eric, turning wearily to his books and files of notes, sitting down at the table, prodding forward his tired, patient brain, already so overburdened with the loads he had put upon it during the last two years—now I must work.

* * * * *

"Is that you, ducky? Come up," shouted Maurice from the top of the stairs.

He was very smartly dressed and rather conscious of it. Eric didn't like his fashionable little double-breasted waistcoat or his pointed shoes. He'd obviously already had a few drinks:

"I haven't seen you for simply *ages*."

"Not since last night," Eric smiled.

"I say, did I really see you last night? So I did, of course. What an idiot I am, aren't I?"

"What did you do with the signpost?" Eric asked.

"It's been in the sitting-room. But Mrs. Brown doesn't like it; do you, Mrs. Brown?" For the landlady had appeared with a tray.

"No, indeed I don't, Mr. Scriven. And I hope you'll take the nasty dirty thing away soon. You'll be getting me into trouble."

"Darling Mrs. Brown, yes, of course we'll take it away if you're really sure you don't like it."

Edward Blake was in the sitting-room, with a woman. Eric was rather surprised to recognise her as a painter whom he'd met once or twice at Aunt Mary's last Vac. Her name was Margaret Lanwin. Aunt Mary was having a show of her pictures at the Gallery. She smiled when they shook hands, as much as to say: I expect you're wondering why I'm here. Eric remembered that he had liked her.

"Edward's been showing me a perfectly marvellous new cocktail," said Maurice. "What's it called, Edward?"

"Satan's Kiss," said Edward Blake.

He had greeted Eric quite warmly, and yet, as Eric always felt, with a sarcastic grin. He looked very ill, iller than ever. His face was streakily grey, as though his cheeks had been rubbed with an india-rubber, and there were sharp lines on either side of his mouth. His big pale eyes were mocking and full of light. His sallow nicotine-stained fingers were mere bones. The signet ring was quite loose on his hand, and Eric noticed how it shook as he lifted his glass.

"Is there any left?" Maurice asked.

"Unfortunately not."

"Well, be an angel and make some more."

"I'm afraid we've used all the Angostura Bitters."

"It won't be quite the same kind of kiss as the last," said Margaret Lanwin.

"No two kisses are alike," said Edward.

As he talked, his mouth gave a nervous sideways twitch and he spoke deliberately, as though he had to concentrate on pronouncing the words. It produced the effect of something said in a foreign language.

Eric sipped the cocktail, which was, he thought, very nasty. It tasted rather like cough-mixture. But Maurice declared it was even better than the last.

"How on earth do you do it, Edward? You are marvellous."

Edward didn't answer. He smiled.

"If it's not a terribly rude thing to say, Maurice," said Margaret Lanwin, "I'm nearly dying of hunger. All those fascinating things on the sideboard are making my mouth water."

"I hope you don't mind all this cold stuff," said Maurice.

But he really apologised to Edward, not to Margaret.

At lunch, Edward ate scarcely anything, although he refused nothing. He drank a great deal —first of College ale, which Eric found terrifically strong; then of brandy, which Maurice produced with cigars. As he drank he seemed to become steadier. His hand no longer shook.

Maurice was telling him about Currie's Sunbeam. "By God," said Maurice, "that was a marvellous bus. You know, Edward, you ought to get a car."

"What does one do with a car?" Edward asked.

"One drives about, of course. I mean, it's miles cheaper when you want to get anywhere."

"But I never do want to get anywhere."

"I'm sure Maurice would exercise it for you," said Margaret, smiling.

She obviously didn't mean to be malicious, but Maurice answered rather shortly:

"I don't quite see what the point of that would be."

Later, Edward did a balancing trick with a

knife, two glasses and an orange. It was not a very difficult trick. The principal wonder lay in Edward's being able to do it. He seemed to hold himself steady by sheer will. And Maurice kept repeating:

"Edward, you are marvellous."

"Can you do this?" said Edward, picking up the knife and addressing only Maurice. He had turned in his chair, away from the others. He slowly opened his fist, until the knife seemed to cling unsupported to the palm.

"How on *earth* do you do that?" Maurice asked, round-eyed.

"Just watch once more."

Edward sat smiling, holding the knife aloft like a snake-charmer. From the tone of his voice, he and Maurice might have been alone together in the room. Eric suddenly glanced at Margaret Lanwin. She smiled back at him.

"No, I haven't an idea. *Do* tell me, Edward."

"Watch once more."

Maurice watched.

"Oh, you might tell me!"

"Do you see how it's done?" asked Edward, suddenly turning to Eric.

Eric felt himself blushing angrily as he answered:

"Yes."

He picked up the knife, holding Edward's faintly mocking gaze with his own. Slowly, awkwardly, he opened his hand.

"Oh, how clever of you!" said Margaret.

"I believe I see how it's done now," said Maurice.

Edward was silent. He only smiled, filled himself another glass of whisky. Eric flushed a deeper red. There was a long pause.

"I ought—it's time I was going," said Eric abruptly.

"Oh, Eric," said Maurice, with sudden concern; "you can't go yet."

But Eric had already risen to his feet. Margaret Lanwin looked at her watch.

"Where can I find out about trains?"

"In the Porter's Lodge," said Maurice. "I'll show you."

But he obviously didn't want to leave Edward Blake.

"Oh, by the way, Edward," he said, "hadn't we better go and see the room I've booked for you? You mayn't like it."

Rather to his own surprise, Eric found himself saying to Margaret:

"If you care to come with me, I can find out about the trains at our Lodge."

She rose at once.

"Thank you very much." Turned to Maurice:

"And thank you very much indeed for my wonderful lunch."

To Edward she said:

"Shall I see you again?"

"Come back here for tea," said Maurice—"the

only thing is, if we don't happen to be here—I mean—you won't mind——?"

Margaret smiled:

"I think I'll go straight to the station; thank you, all the same. I've promised to hold your mother's hand to-night at a ghastly party."

"Give her my love."

"I will. Good-bye and thank you again. Good-bye, Edward. Enjoy yourself."

"I'll endeavour to," said Edward, making her a bow.

Eric followed Margaret out. They walked along the street in silence.

"That's King's, isn't it?" asked Margaret, at length.

"Yes," Eric answered, and added:

"Have you been here before?"

"Once. Ages and ages ago. Before the War."

After they'd talked to the College porter about trains, Eric said:

"I say—if you care to—I'll make you a cup of tea in my room. It wouldn't take a second. And there's no point in going to the station yet."

She smiled: "Thank you very much."

"This is nice," she said, when he had shown her into the sitting-room. She wandered round the shelves, picked up 'Cunningham' and turned over a few pages, tapped 'Stubbs' thoughtfully with her forefinger as if testing its solidity. Eric was a little embarrassed by the strangeness of her presence there. Aware of her semi-bohemian elegance, her aura of sex—for she was very attractive, certainly, although probably somewhere near forty—he got the kettle, filled it, lit the gas-ring on the landing, put his head into the cupboard for cups. When he came in with the tea she was on her knees at the fender, poking up the fire.

"It must be rather a nice life here, I should think," she said; and Eric did not demur, did not even condemn her in his own mind as stupid.

There was a long silence. Then Margaret asked, as if half speaking to herself:

"I suppose you're a great friend of Edward Blake's?"

"I've known him a very long time," said Eric. "He was a friend of my father's."

She did not appear to notice anything in his tone.

"Yes, I see," was all she said.

There was another pause. They talked in a desultory way about indifferent topics. Then Margaret said she must really be going. Eric offered to accompany her to the station. She refused, smiling:

"I've made quite enough of a nuisance of myself already."

III

Eric asked at the office for the number of Mr. Blake's room. Upstairs, in the corridor, he met a maid with a breakfast-tray. The shoes still stood outside several doors. He had not realised that half-past nine might be considered by some people as early. And he wished now that he hadn't brought his books and gown. There was a lecture at eleven. Plenty of time to make a second call at his College. But he had thought: Why should I put myself out? For *him*.

Angrily, Eric was aware of his red hands. Out-of-doors it was cold. And he could feel how untidy his hair was. He smoothed it clumsily, slung his gown over his other arm, dropped his books, cursed, picked them up and knocked at number eleven.

Complete silence. Eric waited, half-raised his hand to knock again, let it fall. He had an almost overwhelming impulse to run away, and might have done so, had not the chambermaid reappeared at the end of the passage. Drawing himself together, marshalling his rehearsed intentions, his pre-arranged attitudes, closing the eyes of his reason, he rapped loudly on the door.

"Come in."

It was quite a small room, and Edward Blake lay in bed, facing the window. He did not turn his head at once, and Eric had a moment's impression of the profile of an invalid—pale, unshaven, staring passively at the daylight. His breakfast stood beside him on a little table, but he seemed to have eaten nothing.

He turned slowly, beginning a yawn which abruptly ended:

"Hullo? Good morning."

He may well look surprised, Eric thought. Answered gravely:

"Good morning."

There was a pause, during which Edward seemed to become fully awake:

"Won't you sit down?"

"I'd rather stand, thank you."

Edward yawned, stretched himself, grinned:

"Do by all means, if you prefer it."

"I'm afraid I'm disturbing you," said Eric, feeling the anger rise within him. "I shouldn't have come so early."

"Not at all."

"I shan't keep you long."

Edward reached a thin, sallow hand out to the table for a cigarette case:

"Won't you smoke?"

"No, thank you."

"As a matter of fact," said Edward, lighting his cigarette, "I'm very grateful to you for calling me. I've got to catch a train up to town to-day."

"I know. That's why I came."

"I see."

"There's s-something"—Eric made a desperate effort to control his voice, but it was loud, hoarse, abrupt, and the stammer seized him—"s-something I must t-talk to you about."

A very faint smile seemed to pass like a shadow over Edward's mouth. He was sneering again. The swine. He exclaimed suddenly:

"I say, I do wish you'd sit down."

Eric made no acknowledgment. He took a chair, curtly, with a certain pleasure that he'd managed to get on Edward's nerves. There was a long silence. Eric was quite calm again now—ready for the attack. But he wasn't going to lose the least advantage. Edward should speak first.

"Well, what is it?"

Eric moved his chair a little.

"It's about Maurice."

A chambermaid passed down the passage with a clinking tray.

"About Maurice?"

"Yes."

Again that shadow of a smile on Edward's face.

"What about Maurice?"

"I think you know quite well." Eric felt the blood suddenly burn hot in his cheeks. He said furiously: "And I'm p-perfectly well aware that it's none of my business."

"Don't let that worry you." Edward openly grinned. "I suppose you came here this morning to tell me to leave Maurice alone?"

"Yes, I did." But Eric, for all his defiance, couldn't help showing surprise.

"You're wondering how I guessed?"

"I suppose all this is just a joke to you."

"I beg your pardon, Eric."

"It's all very well for you to smile. Perhaps you d-don't realise that one person can wreck another p-person's whole life."

Edward stubbed out his cigarette. Took another.

"So you think my influence over Maurice—such as it is—is bad?"

"I think it's about as rotten as it could possibly be."

Edward smiled. Said pleasantly:

"Hadn't you better tell me exactly what it is you object to?"

"You give him presents. You pay for everything. You take him everywhere. You encourage him to rely on you for money. You follow him about. Even when he's up here you can't leave him alone——"

"You know yourself that that isn't true."

Eric disregarded the interruption:

"Perhaps you're not aware that you're the talk of the College?"

"Really?" Edward laughed. "The College must have very little to do."

"That doesn't make it any better for Maurice."

"And what does the College say?"

Eric felt himself blushing again:

"You can imagine."

"And you agree with them?"

"What I t-think"—Eric's voice shook—"is n-none of your business."

There was a pause. Edward blew a puff of smoke from his cigarette. He said mildly:

"I suppose you realise that, in making these insinuations, you're suggesting that Maurice is as bad, or nearly as bad, as I am. After all, he isn't a child."

"He's as weak-minded as one."

"And you can't imagine that there could be a perfectly decent and respectable friendship between two people, one of whom had money and the other hadn't?"

"Of course I can imagine it. But not between you and Maurice."

"Why not?"

"Because you're old enough to be his father."

Edward laughed, but Eric could see that he was taken aback.

"Do I seem so old to you?"

"It doesn't matter what you seem to me"—Eric was contemptuous—"the point is: you are old."

"And even assuming my great age, you don't think it should ever be permitted for an old man to prefer the company of a young one to that of other old men?"

"All I think is," said Eric impatiently, "that you're doing Maurice harm. And so I've come to ask you to leave him alone."

Edward was sitting up in bed now. His hair was ruffled into a kind of crest, making him look like an alertly impudent bird. He asked, smiling:

"And supposing I don't? What shall you do?"

Eric answered gravely:

"I can't do anything."

"You could tell Mary, for instance, what you think."

"She wouldn't understand."

There was a long silence. Edward smoked, smiling faintly to himself. At length he asked:

"I suppose, Eric, I'm the wickedest person you've ever met?"

"I don't think you're wicked. I think you're weak."

Edward grinned broadly.

"You don't blame me too much?"

"I don't blame you at all. What you d-do is no affair of mine."

"So long as it doesn't affect Maurice?"

"Yes."

"But tell me, Eric—this interests me. If I'm not wicked, I suppose you think I'm really a bit mad?"

Eric felt himself go scarlet. He said confusedly:

"I know you had a very bad time in the War."

"So did others."

Eric was silent.

"You think it's about time I pulled myself together?"

"At least"—Eric did not mean it unkindly—"you could make an effort."

Rather to his surprise, Edward smiled:

"Yes, the War's getting a bit old as an excuse now, isn't it?"

Edward dropped the stump of his cigarette into the coffee-cup. Added:

"Well, I'm afraid I can hardly promise to reform myself. But I'll do my best to keep clear of Maurice. Will that satisfy you?"

"If you really mean what you say."

"I give you my word of honour. But, of course, I forgot. I haven't any, as far as you're concerned."

Eric did not reply. Edward continued in a different tone:

"Eric, your father was the only real friend I've ever had. It seems rather silly that we should be enemies."

"I'm not your enemy."

Edward made a grimace.

"I'm afraid that's not saying very much, is it? Well I, at any rate, rather admire you."

"I d-don't want your admiration!" exclaimed Eric in a loud, childish voice. He had risen to his feet. Trembling, furious with himself, he knew that in a moment he would burst into tears. "I m-must be g-going," he muttered. Gathering his books and gown, he made blindly for the door.

"Good-bye," Edward called after him. "And thanks for waking me up."

* * * * *

That evening Margaret was in her studio. There was a terrific postman's knock.

"Thank God, you're in."

"Why, Edward, whatever's the matter?"

He stumbled across the room, collapsed on the divan like a sack. He looked up at her slowly, with an uncertain grin:

"Don't get the wind up. I'm only a bit tight."

Margaret thought that he looked much worse than tight. She said briskly, in a voice she hadn't often used since Red Cross days during the War:

"That's all right. Put your feet up. Shall I make you some black coffee?"

"My God, if you would!"

She hurried into the little kitchen, came back with cups. At first Edward lay with closed eyes. Then he opened them and watched her. She moved briskly. The coffee was soon ready. Surprisingly soon. Margaret was never to be taken unawares. She'd made Edward coffee before.

"Here you are," she smiled.

Edward tried to raise himself on one elbow. Sank back with a groan.

"I'm all done in."

"Let me," said Margaret.

Smiling, she slipped an arm under his shoulder, raised him gently with a strong movement, brought the cup to his lips. Edward drank greedily. Then he lay back. She sat down on the edge of the couch and smiled at him. Edward's gaze cleared.

"Margaret."

"Yes, Edward."

"I want to ask you a question."

"Ask away."

"Why"—Edward brought out the words with his peculiar deliberation—"are you so damned good to me?"

"Am I?"

"You are. Christ alone knows why. Well, I want to know too."

Margaret turned away her eyes.

"Does it matter particularly?"

But she spoke very low, hardly above a whisper. And Edward had made a sudden violent movement, as though he were trying to break a mesh of ropes. He raised himself on his elbow. Almost shouted:

"Margaret!"

"Yes, what is it?"

"Take me away from here."

She smiled.

"Where?"

"Anywhere. Out of this damned town. Out of this cursed country."

"All right."

"You will? You promise?"

"Yes," she soothed him. "Of course."

"How soon?"

"As soon as possible."

"To-morrow?"

"We couldn't start to-morrow."

"But soon?"

"Yes."

"Thank God!"

He raised himself, half turned, let his head sink back into her lap. Looked up at her with a strange, unhappy, boyish smile.

"You really mean it?"

"Of course, my dear. If you really want it."

Edward lay still for a second. Then he said quite distinctly, but half to himself, as though he were perfectly sober:

"I wonder if you can bring it off."

"I'm going to try," said Margaret, and her fingers moved softly through his hair. She couldn't look down at him. Her lips were trembling. The tears smarting in her eyes. So he had said it. At last.

* * * * *

Like a prisoner strapped ready for torture, Eric lay rigid, his fists clenched, in his narrow bed. Liar! he thought. Hypocrite! Liar! Cheat! He stared furiously at the dark ceiling. I was jealous. The whole thing was nothing but jealousy.

I'm ten thousand times worse than Edward, Eric thought. Ten million times worse.

Jealous; jealous; jealous!

I'm not fit to live.

* * * * *

It was more than three weeks later that Eric received a card postmarked from the South of France. A staring blue bay backed by a sky the colour of strawberry ice-cream. The tinting of sea and sky overlapped a little at the edge, staining the horizon puce.

All it said was:

"Please accept this as an alibi.

EDWARD"

* * * * *

Maurice also had received a card. The message was one word shorter:

"This is where I am."

Maurice stuck the card on his mantelpiece after a single glance. He was sorry, but not particularly surprised, to hear that Edward was out of reach.

Edward had promised to take him to Paris next Vac. Very likely he'd forgotten. There was no expecting anything from Edward, and Maurice was much too worried to waste any time thinking about him just now.

A very awkward thing had happened.

Currie had said, once or twice, that Maurice might borrow his Sunbeam when he wasn't there. And so, naturally, Maurice had taken to using it regularly. And, of course, it had had one or two little knocks which the garage people had grinned over and charged to Mr. Currie's account. Apparently he never made a fuss.

And so things had gone on in a very nice friendly way until last week, when Maurice had had the bad luck to run straight through a brick wall when swerving and skidding to avoid some fool on a push-bike. And Farncombe, who'd been with him, had broken his arm and his collar-bone. And Currie had suddenly become quite beastly, which Maurice couldn't understand. He was sorry he'd ever made friends with the man. Worst of all, Jimmy was making a thorough enquiry into the whole affair.

So Maurice had almost forgotten Edward's existence.

* * * * *

Eric's brain, whenever he was not actually working, struggled with the composition of a letter to Edward. He made drafts of it and tore them up immediately. Sometimes it was to be very long. Sometimes very short. What exactly did he want to say? He didn't know.

That letter was never written.

BOOK FOUR

1929

I

THE headlights of the car illuminated a notice on a tree. "Trespassers will be prosecuted." Somebody had cut this with a penknife and scribbled it over with chalk.

Maurice drew on the brake and turning yelled out:

"Wake up, we're here."

Mary stirred comfortably on the back seat and came out of her doze far enough to say:

"Be quiet. We aren't."

"Does one open the gates," asked Edward, "or do we wait for the lodge-keeper?"

"You're the lodge-keeper," said Maurice.

"Why all this excitement?" came Margaret's voice languidly, from the back seat. "Has there been an accident?"

"No," said Edward, "we've reached John o' Groats and Mary's forgotten to bring the bathing-suits."

He opened the door of the car and got out stiffly.

"My God, it's cold!"

"Well, keep it to yourself, my lad," said Mary. "We'll believe you."

Edward shivered. The morning was horribly damp and raw. The gates were clammy and wet. The trees along the side of the road were dripping from every twig. Dawn showed cold and sickly over the Derbyshire hills, dimming the rays from the headlamps.

Just behind, Tommy Ramsbotham's two-seater was panting. Edward walked up to it, put his head inside and said:

"Hullo! Good morning."

"Good morning," said Tommy; and Anne, sitting beside him, asked:

"Did you sleep well?"

"Incredibly."

Edward felt himself suddenly in high spirits. Abruptly, he uttered a short strong laugh, slapped his sides and cut a caper on the wet road.

"Your rear passengers are dead," he added.

There they sat, in the dickey, two shapes stuffed into greatcoats, pullovers, fur helmets, swathed with woollen scarves, resembling very fat owls. Georges had completely sunk into himself, so that you could just see a vast ovoid mass, but poor Earle Gardiner was upright, in a position suggesting how terribly he'd been bumped during the journey.

"Are you all right?" Edward asked.

"Sure, I'm fine," Earle smiled heroically.

Edward put his mouth to Georges' ear and suddenly bellowed:

"*Sept heures moins un quart!*"

Georges woke up without a start and gave him a dazzling smile. Maurice began sounding long blasts on his horn.

"Gates!" he yelled: "Gates!"

Edward pushed them open and Maurice drove through into the park, Tommy following. As they moved off down the drive, Pamela woke up and turned round. The sight of Mary seemed to surprise her. She sat up sharply, in a way which instantly conveyed that not more than a year ago she'd been a schoolgirl, with her innocent head full of abductions and the White Slave Traffic. Then she was properly awake and recognised them all with a grin of relief.

"I must have been asleep," she confessed, with surprise.

Mary was thinking how narrow the drive was and how much smaller the whole park seemed. In less than a minute they were running downhill to the house. Anne, beside Tommy, fixed her eyes on the red spark of Maurice's tail-light. The hood of the two-seater was draughty. She had got a stiff neck. Tommy's profile, as he leant forward to the gear-lever, showed sharp against the pale stretch of land. It was getting lighter every minute. She rested her cheek for a moment against his shoulder.

"What is it?" asked Tommy, his eyes fixed ahead.

Then he realised and slipped one arm round her shoulder as he drove. He would, perhaps, always be a little slow, a few seconds late. My darling. My precious treasure. Feeling the rough tweed against her cheek, Anne spoke in a small dreamy voice:

"She's been running splendidly, hasn't she?"

"Not too badly. It's this new juice. We must stick to it."

Their voices were so warm and intimate with love that they might have been talking of a new-born baby. Gerald's old two-seater, which he'd turned over to Tommy when he got the Bentley. And within a week came the smash. The doctor said that if he'd lived he'd have been a cripple. It was impossible to think of Gerald as a cripple. It made Anne shudder. She'd sometimes felt a sort of hatred of his red beefy health. He was strong and stupid like an animal. And like an animal he had been suddenly and stupidly killed, with a pipe in his mouth, travelling at seventy miles an hour. She'd never forget how Tommy had come to her, that afternoon, straight from the hospital. He had seemed quite dazed. He had to keep telling her exactly what had happened.

"You know, Anne," he kept repeating, "at first I didn't recognise him at all. It might have been a stranger."

And through all her horror—strange, remorseless, as it seemed—she'd felt a curious, new joy, growing up swiftly and secretly in the darkness of her heart. Gerald had done this for her. At last. Within a week of the funeral she'd told Tommy that she loved him.

How queer to think that people could say, almost certainly did say, that she was marrying Tommy for his money. Now they would be rich. Gerald had had everything—Cambridge, holidays at Monte Carlo, money for actresses. And now it would be Tommy's. But all that was merely a joke, so long as Tommy never believed it. And he never shall believe it, Anne promised him.

"Well, here we are."

Edward had opened the garden gates. Swinging on them like an urchin, he waved his hat to Maurice and Tommy as they drove past and round the sundial to the front door. Maurice swerved too sharply, crushing a bit of turf from the corner of the grass with his wheel.

"I'm awfully sorry," he said to Tommy, jumping out. "I've spoilt your lovely lawn."

The others followed stiffly, stretching themselves. Gathered in the shelter of the porch. Edward, having closed the gates, came bounding across the garden towards them.

"How incredible this is," he said to Mary, "I feel as if I'd just arrived for the Christmas holidays."

"Why," asked Pamela, "have you been here before?"

"It was some time ago." Edward grinned.

"Ring the bell, Tommy," said Maurice.

Tommy rather solemnly advanced and rang the bell. They waited. Now that the engines of the cars were stopped, there was a deathly silence. You could hear the trees dripping in the park.

"No one at home," said Edward.

"It's awfully early," said Maurice, as though apologising to some one. Curiously enough, none of them had fully realised this. They looked at each other guiltily.

"I don't suppose anybody's up yet," said Margaret.

"Hadn't we better clear off for a bit?"

"Let's go and knock them up at the Station Inn," suggested Mary.

But Tommy, with a decision which reminded them that he was junior master of the house, merely pressed the bell again. They waited. It was cold.

"Is there any of that beer left?" asked Edward. Mary shook her head. Earle, who'd stayed in the dickey, now climbed out, cautiously, being careful not to disturb Georges, who was sound asleep again.

"What I like," said Edward, grinning with pure glee, "is that you can't hear the bell ring. It's such a long way off. Do you know," he added, turning to Earle, "the bell rings at least a quarter of a mile from here?"

"Is that so?" said Earle politely.

"Don't you believe him, my dear," said Margaret. "He's only taking advantage of your innocence."

"I expect it's out of order," said Tommy.

"You'd much better leave them alone till breakfast-time," Mary said.

But Tommy sternly shook his head. His honour as host was, it seemed, at stake. Mary felt sorry for him. It was really no fault of his, for he'd never suggested this mad expedition. That, naturally, had been Maurice's idea, inspired by Edward. And last night it had certainly seemed amusing to pack into the cars and go racing off through the suburbs, mildly drunk, shouting and singing. One always forgets that car drives take such a long time. Like that awful occasion when Edward had persuaded them to set off at a few minutes' notice for Penzance. They'd ended up in an hotel at Bournemouth, where the food was beneath criticism.

Tommy knocked heavily with the iron knocker. They could hear the hollow echo of the knocking inside the house. No answer.

"This building must be tremendously old," said Earle, in his polite, formal way—so that they all laughed.

"Come away, Tommy," said Anne, laughing.

Tommy, with a smile, knocked four times. A dog began barking somewhere inside.

"Something's begun to materialise," said Edward.

"It's the cry of a *haound*, Watson!" Maurice did one of his stock impersonations. Edward pulled a dreadful face. A bolt inside the door went off like a pistol-shot, making them all jump. They hadn't heard footsteps. The door opened five or six inches on the chain. It was Mrs. Compstall, the housekeeper, who'd been taken over temporarily with her husband from Eric when Ramsbotham bought the house. She had her head in a shawl. She didn't for a moment recognise Tommy.

"What is it?" she asked, her face a blend of aggressiveness and alarm.

"May we come in, Mrs. Compstall?"—Tommy was quite humble now. "I'm afraid it's rather early."

She opened the door with a bad grace, muttering an apology, of which was audible only:—
". . . of course, if we'd been let know. . . ."

They trooped in, a little awkward. Edward recovered first. As the lights were switched on he looked round and exclaimed:

"Welcome to the Hall!"

Mary caught the look of open dislike with which Mrs. Compstall eyed him. And no wonder. She naturally regarded this surprise visit as an attempt to find her out, to catch her red-handed in some sort of unlawful enterprise—baby-farming or a secret distillery. They all stood round, stale-looking in their motoring things, eyeing the dismantled hall. The daylight paled the lamps. The lamps made the daylight ghastly. The whole house felt damp and draughty and freezingly cold. The furniture looked at that hour like ugly, dirty lumber. Catching sight of herself in a mirror, Mary thought: Oh, God! it's not half so dirty as my face.

Pamela came into the hall with a shiver and a timid grin. Could she be the same girl who, nine hours earlier, had put her head on Edward's shoulder? She was a 'cello student at the Royal College.

"Can we have something to eat, please, Mrs. Compstall?" said Tommy, who seemed determined to see this visit through in the right style.

This was almost too much for Mrs. Compstall. She snapped:

"There's nothing in the house."

"We can go and get something in the car," said Maurice, who perhaps thought that he would thus ingratiate himself, "if you'll tell us what to buy."

Again Mrs. Compstall was reduced to muttering:

". . . couldn't undertake . . ."

Tommy surprised them. He was really annoyed. He said:

"In that case, we'd better go."

There was such unmistakable menace in his tone that Mrs. Compstall admitted:

"There's eggs. And you could have coffee, if that would be sufficient."

"That'll be splendid," said Edward.

But Tommy turned to Mary, Pamela and Margaret:

"Will that be enough for you?" He seemed almost to be asking them to say that it wouldn't. They assured him that it would. Mrs. Compstall was looking round, counting the party. At this moment Georges appeared in the doorway, sleek and composed, trailing a muffler along the ground behind him, with his "Aha!" of satisfaction. Mrs. Compstall looked quite alarmed. She asked, in a frankly cowed voice, if they would have their breakfast in the smoking-room. She would be as quick as she could. She hurried away.

"I wonder," said Edward, "if my memory deceives me!"

He walked over to the porter's chair and lifted the padded seat.

"Do you remember," he asked Mary, "the day you first showed me that?"

"Nonsense, my lad. You found it for yourself. I was an exceptionally modest girl."

Maurice had never seen the chair before. He was delighted. He jostled Edward, for they were both trying to sit down at once. Pamela looked slightly shocked. Margaret said conversationally to Earle:

"It's rather touching to think of the poor dear never leaving his post."

"Who?" asked Earle, quite at sea as to what was going on—admiring the pictures.

Maurice was shouting that the cistern was empty. Tommy had begun to laugh in spite of himself, keeping an eye on Anne, hoping she didn't mind. So Anne laughed. And really it was quite funny until Georges made the whole thing heavy and French by roaring out:

"*Ça ne marche pas?*"

"Do you think we might wash a bit?" said Mary to Tommy.

He was all responsibility in a moment.

"Yes, of course; I'm sorry. I'll go and see if I can get you some hot water."

At length breakfast was announced ready. The smoking-room looked very bare. There were three new small tables covered with American cloth. People had been given teas here in the days when the Hall was open to trippers.

Edward asked Mrs. Compstall:

"Has the Squire been over lately?"

She was plainly puzzled. He had to explain:

"I mean Mr. Ramsbotham."

That was really rather unkind, thought Mary, especially in front of Tommy. Edward could be malicious when he liked. Poor old Ram's B. The second Mrs. Ram would do all the squiring for him.

Mrs. Compstall said yes, Mr. Ramsbotham had been over. Mrs. Ramsbotham was somewhere in the South, he'd said, visiting. Of course, Mr. Ramsbotham was always so busy at the mill.

"She's gone to see her people," explained Tommy, rather stiffly. Anne had noticed that he avoided mentioning his stepmother as much as possible. Though he never uttered a word against her. Bitch that she is, thought Anne, with sudden fierceness, remembering how Mrs. Ramsbotham patronised Tommy. Always so gracious, always assuming that he knew absolutely nothing about anything—had no education; always stopping to explain when she talked of county families or restaurants, or art, or places abroad. The way she pronounced Italian names or quoted French made one really in love with the Lancashire accent. Anne had once, after a lunch with Mrs. Ram, suddenly kissed Tommy because he'd made grass rhyme with Bass. How good he suddenly seemed. How honest. How pure in heart.

"It's a pity," said Maurice suddenly, "that Eric isn't here."

It seemed strange that they hadn't remembered him before.

"I suppose," said Margaret, "he's busier than ever nowadays."

"Edward's the only one who sees him," said Mary.

Pamela wanted to know who Eric was and what he did.

"I think that's perfectly ripping," she said,

when Mary had explained. She turned to Edward: "And you've been helping him?"

"Only for the last month. With the Boys' Club."

"It must be fearfully interesting."

"If you like that sort of thing," said Edward; and catching Margaret's eye, he grinned.

"It's the first honest work Edward's ever done in his life," said Maurice.

"We all know what a toiler you are, my lad," said Mary.

Maurice made his injured-innocence face:

"Me? I bet you wouldn't like to swap jobs—snoring away all day at your Gallery."

"But how exactly does one sell cars?" asked Pamela.

"Well——" Maurice loved being asked this. He drew up his elbows on the table, began: "Last Wednesday, for instance . . ." He was really very funny describing how he'd persuaded a rich Nonconformist boot-manufacturer to buy a rather wonky, but handsome-looking, second-hand saloon. And this, thought Anne, was really the story of how he'd always wangled everything out of everybody—out of Mother, out of tradesmen, out of his masters at school. Anne felt a sudden violent pang of love for her brother. There he was, so artful and unprotected and innocent. An artful little boy.

"But surely, Maurice," she asked, "he won't be

very pleased when he finds out what this car's really like?"

"Of course he won't," said Maurice. "Then I shall sell him a new one."

They all laughed, feeling brighter now that the hot coffee was inside them. Out in the garden it was broad daylight. And Mary, looking at the party as they sat round the table, thought suddenly of Father. I wonder if he can see us now, she thought. I hope so.

"You must love this place, Mrs. Scriven," said Pamela, still a little formal with Mary, whom she'd only met once before last night. Georges made a pun. Earle wanted to know the date of the panelling. Nobody could tell him. Maurice suggested that they should go round the house.

They went upstairs. Edward led the way. He'd forgotten nothing.

"Look, Mary," he said, "they've moved that little table that used to stand in the corner."

"So they have," said Mary absently.

She was thinking: How extraordinary that real live people have lived here. For now the house was quite dead. It had died of neglect. It was a show place, like all the others. Mrs. Ramsbotham would probably not bring it back to life. She would like it better dead. She would have garden-parties here and house-parties from the South. She was a climber. Ram's B. would be kept out of the way. He would be an outcast, spending most of his time at the Midland or at his old home with Tommy and Anne. Anne, at any rate, would look after him and put him up when he was too tight to come out to Chapel Bridge. And Mrs. Ramsbotham, with her elegant jokes, would excuse her husband's absence and spend his money. Well, well, thought Mary, it's none of my business.

She questioned Tommy about the alterations they were going to make, and Tommy rather apologetically explained that they were putting in another bathroom, building a garage in the barn, making a hard tennis court. The work would start as soon as Christmas was over.

"Of course," he added, still apologising, "nothing will really be altered—on the outside, I mean."

"I'm sure it'll be a great improvement," she reassured him.

He brightened.

"I'm glad you think so. Of course, we're going to keep everything just the same."

"I guess it must be a tremendous responsibility to own a place like this," said Earle, who was being much impressed.

Edward opened the folding-doors into the drawing-room. The room was nearly dark, for the shutters had been closed. Only one light lit in the chandelier. Edward walked across to the big mirror, regarded himself for a moment, then raised one arm above his head like a Fascist and exclaimed:

"Salut!"

"Whatever did you do that for?" asked Pamela.

Edward glanced at her with his quick impudent smile. He said:

"I'm certain we could produce ectoplasm here."

"What's ectoplasm?"

"It's white. Rather like sago pudding. It usually forms downwards."

Quite seriously, so that they couldn't be sure if he were joking or not, he described a series of experiments with an Austrian medium. He seemed to have read a great deal on the subject. Pamela was thrilled.

"I do think this house is weird. One could quite imagine seeing a ghost here."

They wandered to the window to admire the view. Mrs. Compstall came in, having fetched her husband, who was obviously just out of bed. He repeated that if only they'd known Mr. Thomas was coming, etc., etc. He lingered for a few minutes and then disappeared, evidently feeling that he'd done his duty.

Mary suggested that they should go out into the garden. She had a feeling that she didn't like being in the house. It was old, nasty, suffocating. She hoped that Anne and Tommy wouldn't come to feel the same about it.

On the staircase, Edward announced that the

little eighteenth-century portrait under the window was obviously a trance-picture.

"You turn that face to the wall some evening when you're alone in the house," he said to Mrs. Compstall, "and in half an hour or so you'll find it's turned round again."

Mrs. Compstall looked at him narrowly, scenting a joke.

"I don't know that I should hardly like to," she answered at length, "not if Compstall wasn't here."

Pamela and Maurice were in giggles over this for some time. Maurice was slightly hysterical with fatigue. He began sparring with Edward, mocking him, until Edward turned on him suddenly and they crashed down the staircase, almost head first, and out into the garden, through the gates, away across the park. Maurice, nearly a head the taller, ran like a greyhound, but Edward overhauled him. The others watched from the window, quite fascinated.

"By Jove!" said Tommy, "he can run."

When Maurice, caught, returned slowly, panting, towards the house, Edward was scarcely winded at all. He vaulted the fence at the edge of the park and bounded across the garden to meet them in the porch, his face radiant with energy. Maurice followed, gasping. Edward grinned:

"Honour is vindicated."

Mary noticed how thin his hair was getting. When the forelock was pushed aside you could see the small hollow in the skull where he had had the operation after his motor accident, last winter, in Berlin. It must have been a beastly smash. Mary didn't like looking at it. She asked, smiling:

"Need you give my child indigestion?"

"I'm sorry."

They walked back across the hall and out on to the terrace. The morning was grey and clear, ready for more rain.

"Say, I could look at this view for ever!" exclaimed Earle.

He seemed so innocent, so much of a Red Indian, in his collar buttoned down at the points, standing there, his hands on the mossy wall, gazing out over the valley. But you wouldn't like it if you had to, my lad, thought Mary, looking at him, mooning in his absurd Yankee vision of the sixteenth century, with a mixture of affection and irritation. And she felt—as so often—yes, they are all my children.

They are all my children, she felt—including Georges, who at that moment came placidly into sight at the end of the terrace, in his broad-brimmed hat, spotted bow tie, check suit and liver-coloured boots, having wandered off and explored the barns.

"I 'ave seen ze hen," he announced, beaming.

The Compstalls, it appeared, had kept poultry as a side-line.

Margaret was making a sketch on the back of an envelope.

"Come and see the hen," said Edward.

"Are you coming?" they asked Mary.

"No, children; I think I'll go and sit down. I shouldn't be sorry to get my poor old feet off the ground for a few minutes."

"Lazy old sow!" said Maurice.

"Thank you for them kind words, my child."

Mary entered the house, pausing to light a cigarette. She'd noticed that there was still a moderately comfortable sofa in the drawing-room, and anything was preferable to being out-of-doors on a morning like this. All the same, she had to admit she didn't like being here. It was creepy—probably literally creepy, with black beetles—and damp. The place must be an absolute sponge after all these years without regular fires. As a little girl she'd always felt scared of being alone in this part of the house. Nothing would have induced her to use the front staircase after dark. By daylight it was bad enough. You had always the feeling that there was somebody standing just round the corner above, waiting for you to come up. In the archway to the corridor, where there was a deep shadow. Standing stone-still and waiting. "My God!" said Mary, almost aloud.

"Why, Mother," said Anne, "did we startle you?"

"You did, indeed, for a moment."

"Did you think we were the family ghost?"

They laughed.

"We were just discussing," said Anne, "whether, if we ring up the mill, there's a sporting chance of scoring a lunch."

"My dear!" said Mary, "we can't possibly all descend."

"Father'd like it," said Tommy earnestly, "he's all alone. He'd never forgive me if he heard you'd been up here and I hadn't brought you over."

"Perhaps the others will want to be getting back."

"You won't be late. We can eat quite early. At twelve, if you like."

"But are you sure, really, that it's all right?"

"Perfectly," said Tommy. "We'll just run up to the Post Office in the car. It won't take a quarter of an hour."

So that was settled. Mary gave up the idea of a nap with a sigh. After all, it would be nice to see Ram's B.

They were off down the stairs at once. Mary, at the window, saw Edward and Margaret come strolling across the garden. They were evidently having one of their mysterious private talks. Mary had years ago given up trying to guess exactly how things were going at any particular moment.

Edward looked up and saw Mary. He waved to her mechanically, not altering the tone of his voice as he asked:

"And how's the latest? Is he from Oxford too?"

Margaret nodded:

"I seem doomed to instruct the young."

"Was it his first go?"

"Really, my dear, you presume too far upon my female modesty."

Edward grinned.

II

His hands folded upon his umbrella-handle, his head slightly bowed, Major Charlesworth was borne smoothly upwards in the lift, like a martyr ascending into heaven. At the door of Mrs. Vernon's flat he paused for a moment before ringing, raised his fingers with a humble, saintly gesture to his thin moustache. To-day he felt so little sure of himself that it seemed necessary to rehearse even the half-dozen words he would have to say to the maid.

But it was Mrs. Vernon who opened the door:

"I've been waiting for you."

This afternoon she seemed almost gay. She smiled:

"I've let the maid go out with her young man. We can make tea ourselves."

Actually, there was nothing to do. The tea-things were set out ready on their lace-edged cloth. It was only necessary to bring the kettle to the boil and fill the silver tea-pot. She gave it to Ronald.

He held it like a sacred vessel in a religious mystery. She smiled, pouring in the hot water:

"Be careful of your fingers!"

And when they were seated facing each other across the low table, she said:

"And now, tell me all about Thursday."

On Thursday Ronald had been to a sale at an old house in Essex. She had been unable, at the last moment, to accompany him. Ronald described the remarkable collection of old prints. And there had been a set of chairs he had particularly admired.

"Oh! I do wish I'd been there," she exclaimed.

He wanted to say that without her the sale had lost its interest. That indeed he'd only gone because he knew she would like to hear about it. He answered merely:

"I think it would have interested you."

"I'm sure it would."

She sipped her tea; asked:

"Shall you be going to the meeting on Saturday?"

"I'm not quite certain."

"I shan't go," she said, "unless you'll be coming. When shall you know?"

She smiled, as if challenging his evasion. He coloured a little, but bravely answered:

"I was waiting, really, I meant, to know whether you would care to come."

She smiled at him, quickly, with soft brilliance.

"I often wonder," she said, "how much of my interest in the Past is genuine. I know I should find it terribly dull to go to these places alone."

Ronald felt that his face was betraying him. He murmured:

"One likes to compare notes with someone."

Again she smiled.

"You must promise never to desert me."

She laughed gaily. He laughed. To imitate her was his only protection. Striving to keep his tone light, even gallant, he answered:

"Yes, Mrs. Vernon, I promise."

She poured him out another cup of tea. Looking him smilingly straight in the eyes, without embarrassment:

"There's a favour I've been meaning to ask you for some time."

His heart seemed to swell:

"Yes?"

"I should like it very much if you would call me Lily. May I call you Ronald?"

He bowed his head—could hardly trust himself to speak:

"Yes, please do," he managed to say.

She leant back a little in her chair, lightly yet beautifully dismissing the subject:

"Thank you. It seemed rather absurd to be so formal, now that we are friends."

This brought tea to an end. They sat for some time silent. Ronald was aware of the silence of the lamplit flat, high up in the great building, above the intense crawling movement of the far-away traffic. It was as quiet and isolated as a shrine. Lily sat thoughtfully gazing before her, at her hand with its single pale-shining gold ring. She asked:

"Tell me, Ronald. If you had your life to live again, would you alter anything?"

He considered her question. It was the first time he had ever been asked it. He was unaccustomed to talk about himself.

"I think," he said carefully at length, "I might have been better off in a cavalry regiment. But it was a question of money at the time. It was impossible to live on one's pay."

Perhaps this had not been quite what she had meant, for she said, with a faint smile:

"I suppose everything is so different for a man."

He considered this carefully also:

"Yes, I think it must be."

Lily smiled gaily.

"Men always seem to me so restless and discontented in comparison with women. They'll do anything to make a change, even when it leaves them worse off."

He must have made some faintly deprecatory movement, for she said:

"Oh, yes, they will! You know you would yourself, if you got the opportunity."

She smiled; she laughed at him with a strange

note of opposition, as though holding him back at arm's distance.

"Whereas," she added, "we women, we only want peace."

He did not answer. She pressed him, almost mockingly:

"I suppose you think that sounds very selfish?"

He replied gravely, with a certain dignity:

"I'm afraid I can't believe that you're being quite sincere."

She laughed strangely.

"Perhaps I'm not; I don't know."

There was a silence. He wished he had not said that. It seemed that she had opened some door, only to shut it again. They avoided each other's eyes, and when Lily spoke, it was to change the subject:

"You know something about silver, don't you?"

"Only a very little."

She rose, smiling:

"Have I ever shown you this?"

Opening a cupboard, she took out a box padded with cotton-wool, unwrapped several layers, brought it across to the light of the lamp.

"As a matter of fact," she said, "I'm sure you can't have seen it, because it has been in the Bank since the War. I've only just got it out."

"It's beautiful," he said, turning the shallow, heavy dish over in his hands.

"It's supposed to be Jacobean."

Ronald examined it carefully:

"Yes. I should say it must be very valuable."

"I believe it is. It belonged to my aunt. She gave it me as a wedding present."

Lily thoughtfully put the dish down on the table. It stood there between them. Then she spoke, not sadly, but with a quiet note of wonder, as if to herself:

"How perfectly extraordinary it seems to think that I'm still alive and the dish is still here. It's like something dug up from another civilisation."

He was silent. He feared by the least word to jar upon her mood. She continued:

"The modern idea seems to be that the old people should enjoy themselves and go about just like the young ones. That there shouldn't be any distinction. They should dress alike and talk alike and do their best to look alike."

She paused, gazing into the shadows.

"I think, myself, that happiness belongs to young people. Old people have got memories."

She was so beautiful as she said that, that Ronald might have interrupted, protested, told her that she wasn't old, but young—would always be young. But he was awed by her strange, rapt manner. She spoke dreamily, like one delivering oracles:

"I think that if one has been very very happy for part of one's life, then nothing else matters."

She added, after a moment, as though pursuing the same line of thought:

"I wish you and Richard could have known each other. I think you would have had a great deal in common."

He sat quite silent, could not reply. She smiled. She said quite simply:

"I've sometimes felt that he is pleased we are friends."

* * * * *

The lift slid down its shaft. He had passed out of the flat, it seemed, like a somnambulist; was walking with long strides through the lamplit streets.

Now, at last, he could value, as never before, the beauty of his treasure—their friendship. Walking erect like a hero, swinging his umbrella, he knew himself to be the most fortunate, the most privileged, as the most unworthy of living men. And this great happiness was not realised too late, about to come to an end. It would go on and on. Week would follow week. I shall see her, he thought. I shall speak to her. We shall have tea together. We shall talk.

And to think that only this morning he'd been tormenting himself with ridiculous madman's hopes, schemes, illusions. He had considered his meagre bank balance, his pension, his little flat. Yes, he'd been ready to commit that supreme folly, that insolence. They could never have met again. He saw now that she'd have interpreted his proposal as a sort of treachery, a betrayal of his trust, his honoured position. He was ready to agree now that it would have been a betrayal.

How beautifully she had saved him from that folly, the misery of her refusal. How beautifully she'd indicated what their relationship must be. She must have read his thoughts, for surely her every word that afternoon had been a warning, exquisitely conveyed. How gladly he accepted it. For he knew now that he could be of some small service to her, and that was all he had ever really hoped. It was enough of happiness.

If I had met her as a boy, he thought—not supposing that then things might have happened otherwise, but thinking: If I had met her then, how much better my life would have been. It is women like her, he thought, who raise men from the brutes they are. Without them we could be nothing. She is a saint, he thought. I have known a saint.

* * * * *

Tired, walking more slowly, he stopped at last before a door which seemed familiar. It was his Club. The few fellow-members who nodded to him, as he passed through the smoking-room and sat down in his favourite chair, remarked that Charlesworth was actually a quarter of an hour late. Usually, you could set your watch by him—any of his three dining nights in the week.

III

"AND so I'm taking myself off," Edward wrote, trying to steady his hand against the vibration of the little table. "I rely on you to make the peace with Mary. For God's sake, invent some extraordinarily subtle reason for my departure, and be sure to write and tell me exactly what it is. Then I can send her a Christmas card. The truth is merely that I had a sudden dazzling vision of what it will be like at the Gowers' and at the Kleins', and on New Year's Eve at Mrs. Gidden's. And it was too much for me. Please forgive this, certainly not my last, betrayal."

They were well beyond Hannover; had finished lunch. The sad level plains, unfenced, dotted with woods, rotated smoothly beyond the thick pane curtained with green baize to prevent the least draught. The dining-car smelt richly of the cigars of stout shaven-skulled passengers with student scars on their cheeks. Edward's light impertinent eye surveyed them, his fingers drumming the stem of his glass.

Raising it, he sipped; sucked his pencil, added: "I shall be back early in the New Year."

* * * * *

He lay in the deck chair under the tattered eucalyptus tree. The leaves stirred in a faint breeze puffing over the headland. Looking sleepily down the slopes of the terraced hill writhing with black vine-roots, upon the orange and pink houses clustered round the belfry tower. Every pebble of the gritty hillside showed hard and clear in the intense light. But across the dark blue gulf the low, grey, secret-looking destroyers were almost invisible against the opposite shore. Far beyond, high above the terrestrial horizon, snow-facets of Alpine precipices were printed, like a half-developed photograph, on the dazzling air.

Margaret was standing behind him. She had just come down from the house.

She smiled. Her teeth showed bone-white against the darkness of her sunburnt skin. She was radiant. Her eyes shone.

"Food's ready."

"What is there?" asked Edward, with a big yawn.

"Omelette, fruit, salad—I've tried it the new way Thérèse showed us."

"Splendid."

He rose wearily, weary of sitting still. He'd eaten enough for months. He ate with her eyes upon him, forcing down the mouthfuls. She asked anxiously:

"Isn't it good?"

"It's first-class."

"No, but tell me, the flavouring isn't quite the same—is it?"

He roused himself to consider.

"I believe it needs a little more of that stuff that looks like parsley and isn't—what's it called?"

"Yes. You're right. It does."

That afternoon he'd lain watching her as she stood before the easel. She worked rapidly and decisively, dabbing at the canvas with a sort of triumph, half-smiling to herself. He knew that she liked him to lie near her, on the verandah or under the tree. If he went away by himself, down into the town or across the headland to Pampelonne, he'd find, when he returned, that she'd done scarcely any work. She missed her pet cat.

Yet she was always urging him to make little expeditions. To be independent.

"I believe old Morel is taking his car into St. Rafael to-morrow. Would you care to go?"

"Not particularly. Are you going?"

"Oh, I shall be working."

"You want to get rid of me."

She laughed: "My dear, you know I don't."

"Then come, too."

"Of course I'll come—if you want me."

"Why shouldn't I want you?"

So they stayed at home.

Sometimes Edward felt she'd be quite pleased if he came home drunk. She wanted him to be naughty. She encouraged his evenings out. So Edward dutifully strolled down to the little port with its picturesque fishing-boats, its three cafés and its brothel, which boasted an extremely antique and well-worn indecent film. Sometimes he sat up three-quarters of the night chatting to the painters or playing cards. The thin, delicate, staccato Frenchmen fiddling nervously with their cigarettes, winding themselves up slowly like springs while the others talked, then pouncing into a half second's opening in the conversation with their: "*Je suppose que* . . ." The small, untidy, worried-looking Spaniards, sombre and tragic, yet somehow like hairdressers. The large, lazy Russians with many wives. Scarcely a single Englishman. For that Edward was grateful. Yet he was bored. His boredom was like a nostalgia for the whole world. He was homesick for everywhere but here.

When he spent his evenings up at the villa, Margaret and he sat together on the verandah. They read to each other aloud. Or played poker-patience with two little travelling cases which had pockets for the cards. At twelve o'clock it was bed-time. They kissed:

"Good-night, my dear."

Margaret and Thérèse did all the housework. Edward wanted to help, but she wouldn't let him.

"The women must work and the men must sleep," he said.

She only laughed with her quiet, disconcerting triumph. At times it really angered him. It was like being patted on the top of the head.

He took to bathing. He walked down to Pampelonne, the great wild beach littered with bleached sea-rubbish, like bones. The currents were dangerous. In perverse moods he punished her with anxiety. Every morning he did exercises on the verandah; lay outstretched, crucified, drinking in the sun with his naked body. His skin turned to darkest bronze. Stark naked, with furious ironic energy, he performed his comic religious ritual of strainings, stretchings and heavings. Margaret watched him, smiling. And when he saw her looking at him, he felt suddenly ashamed of himself.

Then he went out sailing with the son of the lighthouse-keeper. Often they were away from early morning till sunset. Margaret would come down to the port to meet them.

"I should like to do a picture of Mimi," she said one day.

"Why?"

"He's such a magnificent type. Really beautiful, of his kind. Like an animal."

"Is he?" Edward felt irritated because quite unreasonably guilty.

"Really, Margaret," he added, with his most

unpleasant smile, "you describe people like a nursery governess at the National Gallery."

But after this he didn't go out with Mimi any more. Another boy, named Gaston, was only too glad to take his place. Gaston had a squint.

A few days later Edward asked if she'd mentioned the portrait.

"No, I haven't."

"Why not? I'm sure he'd be delighted."

As a matter of fact, Mimi had been rather attracted by Margaret. He found an excuse to call at the villa. Edward told him, in front of Margaret, about the picture. He was very much flattered. And, of course, after this, Margaret had to do it. Edward thought it the worst thing she'd ever painted. It was bold, cheaply attractive. One day, coming back to the house, he found she'd hung it in his bedroom. He got really angry:

"I wish you'd take that damned thing away!"

And so it was finally presented to Mimi himself. Presumably it occupied a place of honour in the lighthouse.

* * * * *

At length, one evening, Margaret said:

"Edward, how much longer do you want to stop here?"

"Where would you like to go?"

"I didn't mean that. I meant—I know sometimes you like to be alone. You mustn't ever feel tied."

"But aren't you happy here?" he asked uneasily.

"Of course—so long as you are."

Nothing more was said. A few days later she told him:

"Edward, next week I'm going to Paris."

He accepted this. Alone, he was able to stand the villa for two days. Then he left for Marseilles and so by boat to Constantinople. In the autumn he was back again in Paris with a slight fever. They met. He said:

"You see, I fly to you when I cut my finger."

She laughed.

"My dear, that's what I wish."

* * * * *

But they were happy together. They went everywhere, playing a game that they were Americans seeing Paris for the first time. They bought horn-rimmed glasses and conversed in what they imagined to be Yankee accents. The joke collapsed rather feebly, however, when they met an extremely nice sculptor from Carolina and had to explain their behaviour.

Soon they crossed to London. Margaret settled at her studio. Edward took a flat. They went out everywhere together—were always invited as a married pair. They made endless jokes about this —particularly Margaret. Mary was really the funniest. Her discretion, her unobtrusive air of giving her blessing, was really funny.

Margaret said:

"Mary's so sweet. She's really awfully innocent."

She added:

"Ah! Edward—if they but knew you as you are."

This kind of joking made him uneasy. She struck the wrong note; her humour was always slightly strained. They avoided being alone together. At parties they were very bright, playing up to each other like trained actors.

At the villa they'd already discussed what Edward described as "our duty to our neighbours." As he'd said: "Of course, we must try it one day. One never knows. It might be a success." And Margaret had laughed: "To think, Edward—I might cure you."

And so one evening, at the studio, after a particularly hectic party, they'd started—and it had been really very funny and not in the least disgusting—but quite hopeless. They sat up in bed and laughed and laughed. "Oh, Edward!" laughed Margaret—for she was pretty tight, too—"I shall never be able to sleep with a man again. At the critical moment I shall always think of you."

"I might return the compliment," said Edward.

* * * * *

In the spring they went south again, stopping

several weeks in Paris. They hadn't been very long at the villa before news came of the General Strike. Edward wanted to return at once.

"But what would you *do*?" she asked him, half impressed, half amused.

"I don't know. But I want to be mixed up in this."

He didn't even know which side he'd be on. She laughed at him. He was as angry as a boy.

"You don't understand," he said. "Something important is happening. There may be a revolution. And you want me to sit here, hiding in this damned country."

"Why not admit, my dear, that you're simply bored?"

This stung him. It was partly true. Partly—like all women's wisdom. He meditated leaving her. If she'd tried to stop him he'd certainly have done so, but she was too cunning. The days passed. At length came a letter from Mary, making the whole thing seem, of course, a tremendous joke. Maurice had driven an engine. She and Anne had worked at a canteen. The letter ended:

"We all missed you. You would so have enjoyed it."

"I feel quite sorry," said Margaret, "that you didn't go, after all."

The summer passed. The port was infested with painters. Edward sailed, swam, lay in the sun. Margaret didn't offer to paint any more Mimis, but often he had the impression of being ironically watched. Sometimes the whole situation would seem quite impossible; then, the next day, so simple that one couldn't imagine whatever had seemed wrong. According to Margaret's favourite phrase:

"I can't see that anything's unworkable, if people are really honest with each other."

That infuriated Edward. One day he would retort—yes, but who's being honest?

When the weather began to get cooler, Margaret said:

"Why don't we ask Olivier here?"

Olivier was one of their Paris friends. A young ballet dancer.

"Why should we ask him?"

"Only that I thought you liked him."

He'd found himself, in spite of all control, blushing.

"At any rate, I know quite well that you don't."

Margaret laughed.

"My dear, wherever did you get that idea from? Besides," she added, "what on earth has it to do with me? Are we to cut each other off from our friends?"

"I don't notice," he said maliciously, "that you bring your friends here such a lot."

"My friends?" she smiled. "I haven't any."

There it dropped for the moment. But she returned to the attack a few days later:

"Edward," she said, "I wish you'd ask Olivier here."

His temper was not at its best. The mistral had been blowing all day, so that every window in the villa banged and grey clouds of dust swirled up from the town. And Edward's friend, the chemist, had run out of his supply of powders which he administered to chronic sufferers from the weather. Edward flashed a look at her:

"What makes you think I'm pining for Olivier?"

She was a little cold in her reply, as if dealing with an ill-mannered child, but patient:

"I never said you were 'pining'. I merely know you well enough to know that you sometimes require other kinds of company than mine. So I suggest Olivier."

"And what," he said, "do you mean exactly by 'other kinds of company'?"

"I mean what I say."

"How typical it is," he said, "of a woman, that she can never stop reminding people of their obligations."

"I don't understand."

"Well, then, I'll put it more plainly. You regard me as married to you."

"Edward—you can't be serious!"

"But I won't stand it—do you hear? I won't have you sneering at me."

The quietness of her reply suggested that she regarded him as a mere invalid:

"You simply aren't thinking what you're saying."

He looked at her for a moment, with his quick *méchant* smile. Then he said:

"I think you might spare me the final humiliation of being pimped for."

She went out of the room.

Later they made it up. Edward took refuge behind exaggerated surrender. It was his liver. It was the mistral. He hadn't meant a word. She shook her head sadly:

"No, my dear. Don't say all that. You did mean some of it."

There was a pause, and she added:

"And perhaps you're right. Perhaps I sometimes am a bit—possessive."

He protested. She said:

"I sometimes wonder if all this is workable. The way we live."

"It's worked, hasn't it?"

She smiled sadly.

"Has it?"

"You mean, for you, it hasn't?"

"Oh, I'm satisfied," she answered quickly.

"Then you oughtn't to be," was on the tip of his tongue. He didn't say it. Like a coward he avoided, as always, the final issue between them. That evening they were gentle with each other, but sad. He was polite and she accepted it. Next morning she told him that she was going to England in a few days' time. As before, she spared him the unpleasantness of being the one to make the move.

* * * * *

"I believe I have overcome this difficulties," said the young Dutchman, in his incorrect conclusive English, tapping the ash from a small cigar and glancing without interest across the Place de l'Opéra. He was pale and rather stout. Edward nodded seriously and ordered another absinthe. The Dutchman drank only lemonade.

A week later they had left Paris. The experiments were being made at a village not far from Beauvais. The Dutchman had invented a new type of aeroplane engine. He was working as cheaply as possible, but had run out of cash. It was only a matter of a few hundreds. Edward telegraphed to his bank. To Margaret he'd written in a mood of unashamed enthusiasm: "I really believe that this is the genuine Resurrection from the Dead. It's extraordinary, after all these years, to be of some slight use. I only wish I hadn't forgotten all the engineering I ever knew. But even that is coming back by degrees."

Margaret answered warmly, handsomely. He could read between the lines that she was anxious. But she talked gaily of the future. Perhaps Edward would be quite famous.

Everything went splendidly. The French Government was interested. The experts were coming to visit them in a few weeks' time. Two or three reporters appeared, lurked about for a day or two, and were finally driven off, disappointed. The days passed quickly in long hours of work, in discussions, in trial flights. Edward found that his nerve hadn't gone. He was cutting down his drinking. He felt ten years younger.

The Dutchman was killed one morning while flying alone, a few days before the experts came. An elementary piece of carelessness on the part of one of the mechanics. A strut broke in mid-air. The machine side-slipped and was burnt to a tangle of wires within a few minutes of striking the ground. All that Edward could do was to make an idiotic plunge into the flames, attempting to reach the pilot's seat. They barely rescued him alive.

"I'm going to carry on," he told Margaret two months later, when he came out of hospital.

"I only wish I could help you more," she said.

But it was not so simple. There was a legal difficulty, it seemed, as to the ownership of the plans. Edward, of course, had made no business arrangement. Some relatives arrived from Amsterdam and carried them off. Edward raved for a week, talked of going to law, wrote furious letters. Margaret made no comment. They both knew that he could do nothing.

* * * * *

A month later, and he was out of Europe. His first destination was Damascus, but he could rest nowhere. Kerkuk, Suliemaniyeh, Halabja. He shot in the mountains. Paid a visit to Sheikh Mahmoud in his cave. In Halabja he nearly died. He had blood-poisoning in the left hand and arm.

When he got back, late that autumn, to London, he told Margaret:

"I'm getting old. That was the last time. I shan't run away again."

* * * * *

One should never say such things. Next summer, in Paris, he'd met Mitka.

A month passed. On the impulse, he wrote one day to Margaret, who was still at the villa. She must come up and visit them. Rather disconcertingly, she answered that she would.

Edward had found a studio in the Rue Lepic. Margaret admired it, smiling, while he made tea.

"You've no right to a place like this, my dear," she said.

Edward answered that he'd have to take up sculpture to justify his existence. They spoke French. Margaret had tactfully started it. But Mitka wouldn't be drawn into saying a word. He just sat, watching them, and occasionally—with a furtive movement—pushing the lock of fair hair away from his eyes. Her faintly amused smile explored everything. She asked:

"Who mends your socks?" and

"Which of you gets the breakfast?"

At last Edward couldn't stand it any longer. He packed Mitka off brusquely to the cinema, with twenty francs. And Margaret looked on at this little performance, smiling.

They were alone. Staring out of the window, frowning, with his hands in his pockets, Edward asked abruptly:

"Well?"

"Well what, my dear?"

Edward's frown tightened.

"What do you think of him?"

"I think he's charming," said Margaret sweetly.

It was just beginning to rain. Edward turned wearily from the wet pane, crossed the room slowly, sat down on the divan:

"I suppose I was a fool to have asked you here."

"By that, my dear, you mean that I was a fool to have come."

"No."

"I must admit," said Margaret, "that it was largely out of curiosity."

"And you've been disappointed."

"Is my approval so essential to your happiness?"

"On the contrary."

"Well, then——?"

"The truth is," said Edward, with his quick, unhappy, malicious little smile, "you wanted to be quite certain that the exception really did prove the rule."

Margaret asked, with a sigh:

"Need we discuss this?"

"It seems to me that we might as well. For once."

She was silent.

"But tell me, Margaret, this interests me. What have you got against Mitka?"

"That child? I barely noticed him."

" 'That child?' " He mimicked her voice. "You're starting to show off, my dear."

"Well, perhaps I am, a little bit," she grinned; "but I'm really and truly not saying one word against—Mitka? What a pretty name."

"Very. You mean you think this kind of thing is always a failure?"

"No, I don't say that. Not always." She hesitated. "Not for everybody."

"But for me?"

"Yes, Edward, I admit I do think that."

There was a silence. Edward cleared his throat slightly; asked in a different, softer voice:

"Why?"

"I don't know. It isn't your style. It's so——" she paused suddenly, uncontrollably laughed.

"Oh, Edward, I'm sorry, but I just can't *see* you——"

"I wish you'd tell me the joke."

"There isn't a joke. Or, at least—yes, I can't help it, it *is* funny—it's like——"

"What?"

"Like being a nursery governess. Or a responsible private tutor."

"Thank you."

"I'm sorry, Edward. You made me say it, you know. But it *is*. I think one would have to have absolutely no sense of humour. You've got far too much."

"Perhaps not so much as you imagine."

"My dear, you're not angry with me, are you?"

"No."

"You are."

"Not in the least. I'm very much interested."

Again she sighed.

"Gracious! it's late. I must be going."

He followed her down the flights of stairs.

"My dear," she said suddenly, "you know I hope I'm wrong."

"I'm certain you hope you're right."

They parted smiling. Edward grinned, made his little bow. But he hated her. Really hated her. Taking hold of himself, clenching his will into a hard fist of obstinacy and hatred, he slowly climbed the stairs to the studio to wait for Mitka.

* * * * *

One evening, nearly seven months later, Mitka left the studio. He was going downstairs, he said, to the café for a packet of cigarettes. Edward had not been much surprised when, after three hours, he had not returned. Yet he couldn't sleep. He could seldom sleep nowadays until he was pretty drunk. He sat up three-quarters of the night becoming so.

Next morning Mitka wasn't there. That evening Edward went down to the Rue de Lappe. He did not come back to the studio until the afternoon of the next day.

On the third day he telephoned to the hospitals and the police. But Mitka had not been arrested or injured. He was simply gone.

Gone. So it's happened at last, Edward had thought, in the instant before losing consciousness, after his crash in Flanders. Thank God!

* * * * *

Within a week he was getting out of the boat-train at Victoria, gloriously tight. "I'm never going to be sober again," he told Margaret. "Never, never again." She had looked scared. They had all looked slightly scared of him. Rabbits. He wasn't going to hurt anyone. What a comic little town London was. He went to their rabbit parties and played at being a rabbit—the biggest rabbit of them all. People who didn't know him were charmed. His friends were very bright and friendly and a trifle scared.

But this was all temporary. It couldn't go on, and he knew how it would end. At last he had got to be alone. But not here. Not in Paris. Someone mentioned Berlin. He'd taken it for an omen. In forty-eight hours he was on his way.

* * * * *

And that was a year ago.

Edward's brilliant forlorn eyes looked out from the warm, lighted dining-car into the cold brief afternoon world. Twilight was gathering on the huge revolving disc of the plain. The passengers were going back to their compartments. Not long to wait now. His mouth twitched into a little nervous grin. He picked up his pencil. He'd suddenly thought of something funny to write to Margaret.

IV

Mary rang the bell. Lily herself opened the door of the flat.

"Why, Mary! This is a surprise!"

"Good afternoon, Lily. How are you?"

After a moment's hesitation they kissed.

"Very well, thank you. Come in."

Mary followed Lily into the grey and silver sitting-room, admiring the condition in which everything was kept.

"Sit down, won't you?" said Lily, smiling, pushing forward a chair.

"May I look round a little, first?"

"Of course. Why, you've never seen the flat—have you?"

"No—may I?"

They smiled at each other. Lily, smiling with sudden childish pleasure, opened a door.

"This is my bedroom."

Over the bed hung a water-colour of the Hall as seen from the end of the garden.

"I've never seen this before," said Mary.

"Richard did it."

They stood together in silence looking at the picture. Then Lily quietly moved away:

"And this is the bathroom."

"I see you've got the shape of bath I've always wanted."

"Yes, it's quite comfortable."

"And what a nice shade for the light."

"Do you know who sent me that the other day? Mrs. Beddoes."

"Really? Where is she now?"

"She's gone back to her married daughter in Chester. Her son-in-law has a lamp shop, she says."

They moved into the little kitchen.

"I wish I'd known you were coming," said Lily; "I wouldn't have let the maid go out. But really, when I'm alone, there seems no reason for her to stay in. I generally have a cup of tea by myself in here."

"Well, then," said Mary, "let's have it here together."

"Oh, yes, let's! How nice."

"May I take off my coat, and I'll help you?"

"Of course."

Smiling, Lily took plates from the rack. Mary cut bread and butter. Lily heated the kettle on the ring. Mary fetched the teapot. Lily watched.

"Is that how you warm the pot?" she asked.

"Yes. It prevents it from cracking."

"Oh! what a good idea. I should never have thought of that. I must remember it."

They sat down. Mary sipped the tea with relish. It was better than she could afford. And how Lily wasted it!

"I really came here to thank you," she said, "for Anne's wedding present. She'll come herself as soon as she's back in London, but she's staying at the Ramsbothams' just now."

"Yes, she wrote and told me so."

"Really, Lily, it was most awfully good of you. It'll be quite the show piece at the wedding. We shall have to hire a detective to watch it."

Lily smiled: "It was in my aunt's family."

"A friend of ours from the British Museum saw it the other day. He says it's Jacobean."

"Yes."

"You know, you really shouldn't have——"

Lily smiled. And suddenly she was no longer young. There were crow's-feet round her eyes. And her throat drew tight, a trifle skinny.

"I thought Anne might like to have it."

"You should have kept it for Eric."

Lily smiled.

"I sometimes think," she said, "that Eric isn't going to marry."

"Maurice always says that too," Mary laughed.

But she never felt quite comfortable with Lily on the subject of Eric.

"Please tell me about the wedding."

"Well—it's to be at Chapel Bridge."

Lily's eyes lighted up.

"Oh, I'm so glad!"

"And Maurice is to be Best Man. So we're keeping it all in the family."

"And have you fixed the date yet?"

"Not exactly. But some time in February."

"And what will Anne wear?"

Mary went into details. Lily was delighted.

"I'm so glad it's going to be a nice grand affair. Nowadays the weddings seem so plain and informal."

Mary couldn't help smiling, thinking of her own. She said:

"And of course you'll come?"

"Shall I? Really?"

"But, of course, you must support me. I can't face the second Mrs. Ramsbotham alone."

Lily laughed, with childish pleasure.

"Yes, I think I really must."

* * * * *

"Well, you know," said Mary after a pause, "I really must be getting along."

"Oh, must you?" Lily's face fell. "I suppose you're very busy."

"I've got a good deal to do over Christmas. The children will both be at home."

She paused at the door; added:

"You know, Lily, we should be awfully glad

to see you if you cared to come round any time."

Lily smiled:

"It's very kind of you. But I always feel you've so much to do."

"I'm afraid my house is rather a bear-garden. But I tell you what—you've never been to the Gallery, have you? Do come one day, soon. The light's almost gone at four, and we can have a quiet cup of tea all to ourselves without being disturbed. I've at last managed to get the place fairly decently heated."

"I should love to."

"Well, don't forget. Here's the address."

"I'll come as soon as Christmas is over."

"Well, good-bye. Thank you so much for my tea."

"Thank you for coming."

"Good-bye, Lily."

"Good-bye, Mary."

They kissed.

* * * * *

Riding home on her bus, Mary had Lily's figure still before her—the thin, pale, blonde woman bravely smiling at the door of her lonely flat. Poor old Lily. What would she do at Christmas?

That afternoon she'd suddenly had an idea. Why not a show of Richard's and Lily's water-colours at the Gallery? People still bought that sort of 1910 stuff, and it'd make a change. But no, most likely Lily wouldn't hear of it. She wouldn't want to sell. Better not to mention the subject.

It was queer, but to-day she kept thinking of Desmond. Sometimes she forgot him for weeks on end. Perhaps I'm not well, Mary thought. She'd never felt better. Yes, deep down in her bones she felt a power. She was powerful and old. The Future didn't worry her, and she had done with the Past. The Past couldn't hurt her now. And yet, thinking of it all—thinking of Dick and of Father and Mother and of Desmond—of all that had happened, there seemed so incredibly much and everything so complicated and so difficult that if, when she was a girl of fifteen, somebody had brought her a book and said: Look. That's what you've got in front of you, she'd have felt like an examination candidate confronted with a preposterous schedule: But I can't possibly manage all that! And yet it had been managed, down to the very last item; and, after all, it had been easy and not specially strange or exciting. And how soon it was over!

* * * * *

"Mary as Queen Victoria," shouted everybody that evening at the Gowers', after the concert.

"But you must all have seen it."

"We all want to see it again."

"Very well," said Mary, smiling; "since you're all so kind. But this is really and truly the very, very last performance on any stage."

"Liar!" Maurice shouted.

V

EDWARD sat at the table by the window of his room, overlooking the trees and the black canal and the trams clanging round the great cold fountain in the Lützowplatz. It was quite dark already. The reading-lamp lit up the gleaming white tiles of the stove, on top of which was perched a metal angel holding a wreath. Edward lit a cigarette and opened the two letters which had arrived by the afternoon post.

He read Margaret's first:

"I could think of no 'subtle' reason, so finally ended by telling Mary all, without disguise. It worked much better than I expected. In fact, I don't think she was at all seriously aggrieved. I remarked: You know what Edward is, and she agreed that we all knew what you were. You may be thankful, my dear, that we don't.

"Well, the Festival seems to be upon us and this shall be my Christmas letter. I am feeling Christmassy this evening, in spite of a wretched drizzle. And so let me wish you (and myself too) the very best of the Season, and may we both enjoy ourselves according to our own tastes and in our own ways.

"My dear, I feel as though I were very near to you to-night. And I'm curiously happy. (The truth is, I was at a cocktail tea at Bill's studio. But let that pass.) Somehow, I feel awfully secure. About us two, I mean. All our little escapades and adventures suddenly seem so completely trivial beside the fact that we've got each other. Yes, Edward, whatever happens, that stands firm. And it's all that matters. And now I am quite certain that as we get older this will grow stronger and stronger between us and the other thing become less and less important. When I look back over the last year, I see how this has been happening. And, believe me, it will go on happening.

"A merry Xmas, with my dear love, and good-night, my dear."

Edward picked up the other letter:

"Dear Edward,

"This is to thank you for your most handsome subscription to the Club. I wish you could be here in person to help us with our Christmas Party. I think it will be a success.

"There is something I should have told you if I'd known you were meaning to leave London. I am going to become a Catholic. Perhaps this will surprise you. It would have very much more than surprised me a year ago. I don't know exactly when I shall make my first Communion, but it will be soon. Until that is over I shall say nothing to Mary or to my Mother, but I wanted you to know. It is impossible for me to say much about it. I don't propose to try to convert you by describing how it happened. Only I have the most extraordinary feeling of peace. And you who know me will know what a lot that means. Needless to say, I shall carry on with the work here.

"My best wishes for Christmas and the New Year. ERIC"

* * * * *

A long whistle sounded from the darkness of the trees by the canal bank. Edward rose from his chair, pushed open the window, peered down:

"Franz?"

"Edward?"

"Look out."

Edward took the key of the flat from his pocket, let it fall.

"Good. I've got it."

A moment later, and the door opened.

"Well, Edward, you old house, how goes it?"

Franz took off his overcoat, coat and scarf. Then he went, as usual, to the glass and carefully parted his hair with a pocket comb. After this he poured water into the basin and washed his hands.

"How goes it?" Edward asked.

"Bad."

"Been having another quarrel with your step-father?"

Franz nodded, uttered a sudden animal sound like a laugh and performed three rapid handsprings on the back of the sofa.

"Wonderful," Edward mocked. He picked up a paper-knife from the table; asked:

"Can you do this?"

"No. How do you do it? Show me."

"It's quite simple."

"No. Show me. Do it again."

"What's that?" asked Edward, to change the subject, pointing to a long scar on Franz's arm.

"That was last May. At my sister's. The police broke one of our windows with machine-gun bullets."

"Are you a Communist, then?"

"No, of course not."

Franz laughed. Asked suddenly:

"You've got a scar, too."

Edward was rather startled. He didn't think it showed.

"How did you get that?"

"I shot myself."

"You mean, you had an accident?"

"No. On purpose."

"Where?"

"Here in Berlin."

"When?"

"Last winter."

"Why aren't you dead?"

"Because the German doctors are very clever. That's where they dug the bullet out."

Franz laughed. Edward smiled:

"Don't you believe me?"

"Of course I don't."

"Why not?"

"Why should you shoot yourself? You've got money."

His flickering attention moved about the room, fastened on the letters. He examined them with interest:

"Erich? Is that your friend in London?"

"Yes."

"And these are both written in English?"

"Yes."

"Read some of this one. I want to hear how it sounds."

Edward, faintly smiling, read aloud:

" 'In fact, I don't think she was at all seriously aggrieved. I remarked: You know what Edward is, and she agreed that we all knew what you were. You may be thankful, my dear, that we don't.' "

He paused, asked:

"Well, did you understand it?"

"A little."

"What?"

"There's a bit about something being expensive, isn't there? Doesn't 'dear' mean expensive?"

"Yes."

"You see? I can understand English."

Franz smiled complacently, helped himself to a cigarette:

"No, but tell me, Edward. How did you really get that scar?"

"I've told you."

"No. But really. Wasn't it in the War?"

"Yes, if you like."

"You fought in the War?"

"Yes."

"Did you kill many Germans?"

"Quite a lot."

"Then I shall kill you," said Franz, catching Edward by the throat. But he became serious almost immediately:

"It must have been terrible."

"It was awful," said Edward.

"You know," said Franz, very serious and evidently repeating something he had heard said by his elders: "that War . . . it ought never to have happened."